LIONS · TEEN TRACKS

The Undertaker's Gone Bananas

Bobby Perkins knew the minute he saw his new neighbour, Mr Hulka, that there was something odd about him. This was hard to explain, because so much of Mr Hulka's appearance was attractive and his voice was low and mellifluous. Yet something made Bobby determined to keep an eye on him.

One day, Bobby, watching Mr Hulka's apartment from the adjoining balcony, sees Mr Hulka kill his wife. But no one will believe Bobby's story. Not the police. Not the doorman of the 30-storey apartment building. Not even his closest friend, Lauri Geddes, believes what Bobby tells her about Mr Hulka, until the moment when the self-confessed undertaker really goes bananas with a hammer in his hand . . .

In this murder mystery, Paul Zindel has written a *grand guignol* thriller that pivots on an unusually warm and loving relationship between a teenage girl and boy.

D1513428

Also available in Lions Teen Tracks

Paul Zindel

The Undertaker's Gone Bananas

LIONS · TEEN TRACKS

This book is *not* dedicated to the
wicked, wee devils, monsters and
nightmares who stalk us all, but to the
children who so often keep them at
bay using the simple light of their
smiles and their rather reasonable need
to be loved.

First published in the USA by Harper and Row Inc., 1978
First published in Great Britain
by The Bodley Head 1979
First published in Lions Teen Tracks 1980
Seventh impression February 1989

Lions Teen Tracks is an imprint of
the Children's Division, part of
the Collins Publishing Group,
8 Grafton Street, London W1X 3LA

Copyright © 1978 by Zindel Productions Incorporated
All rights reserved

Printed and bound in Great Britain by
William Collins Sons & Co. Ltd, Glasgow

Conditions of Sale
This book is sold subject to the condition
that it shall not, by way of trade or otherwise,
be lent, re-sold, hired out or otherwise circulated
without the publisher's prior consent in any form of
binding or cover other than that in which it is
published and without a similar condition
including this condition being imposed
on the subsequent purchaser

Chapter 1

Bobby Perkins knew the minute he saw Mr Hulka there was something a little wacky about the guy. It was hard to pinpoint exactly what it was because so much of Mr Hulka's appearance was attractive except of course for the part of his face which seemed to be made of Silly Putty. He looked a little like a character actor, only about thirty, but the kind that one knew was never going to make it past doing walk-ons on some awful television show. That first day Mr Hulka was wearing an impressive dark suit and his shirt was stark white with the collar just perfect and a tie hanging down like a stiff knife pointing towards his belt and he had a handkerchief popping out of his jacket pocket. The handkerchief curved at all the right angles like well-fashioned secrets. Actually Bobby decided Mr Hulka came off as perfect casting for his family's first neighbour on the twenty-fourth floor of the fancy Century Tower Apartments. Of course not all the apartments were fancy; there were a few studio apartments but in general the place was so expensive most of the floors weren't even rented yet and it had been open over a year. Bobby thought maybe most people didn't want to move in because the building was erected so close to the edge of a cliff in Fort Lee, New Jersey, that it looked like it was going to fall right over and take the George Washington Bridge with it. One day there would be this great big splash and that would be the end of the Century Tower Apartments and maybe the World Trade Centre as well.

Mr Hulka was being moved into 24G. Bobby and his mother and father lived right next door in 24H, and none of the other eight apartments on the twenty-fourth floor had been rented yet. In fact nobody had rented anything on the twenty-third floor or the twenty-second. There was some man with a collie living on the twenty-first and then there were a few of the penthouses way up on the thirtieth floor that were rented. Aside from that most of the people lived below the twentieth floor. There had been so many fights with the landlord about garbage pick-ups and rent rip-offs and deals under the table that the building had got a terrible reputation and was in the middle of a big court battle because the owner was some money-grabbing villain who didn't care about giving people the services they were promised. Bobby's mother and father had already told him that whoever would move into the G apartment would have to be very rich because it was a huge layout with three bedrooms, a maid's room, a private laundry-room, and a forty-three-foot living-room with terrific views and a wraparound terrace that offered views of Manhattan, the George Washington Bridge, Nyack and if you leaned far over you could even see the Blue Mountains way out in New Jersey. Of course Bobby knew the layout of 24G very well because many a time just to get a little peace and quiet he would sneak under the partition of his terrace which would bring him on to the terrace of apartment 24G, and then he would just open the terrace doors and roll around, sometimes singing songs so they would echo and vibrate off the walls of the empty rooms.

Bobby kept pretending to take things out to the incinerator the entire day Mr Hulka and his belongings were being moved in. Bobby thought Mr Hulka's moving crew looked like a trio of pre-humanoid creatures. They looked like the kind of guys who would come up out of ships' holds where they would stoke furnaces with coal and sometimes be referred to as hairy apes. Mrs Perkins could not understand why Bobby wanted to keep running out with little pieces of garbage, and sometimes Bobby would just stay in the incinerator room until he could hear a little action going on in the hall. Then he would dash out and see what new objets d'art were being carted into 24G. He saw some elegantly carved chairs and cabinets being carried in. A lot of them were made of heavy wood. Some were gilded as though they had just been yanked over from some Transylvanian castle. There were a lot of boxes and two of the weirdest elephant-shaped end tables which looked very cheap, as though they had been made in a substandard Tijuana straw factory. But most of all, there was Mr Hulka – Mr Hulka who moved swiftly, supervising all the little hairy apes, his voice commanding them, making them move faster, carry heavier loads, making them actually stagger from the elevator to his newly rented sanctuary at the end of the hall. Bobby heard Mr Hulka's voice. It was low and smooth and deep and yet there was never any question that he was pulling the strings. He kept those brutes moving with very precise words. In fact, Bobby decided if he had to cast this man in some major role, he would probably get the title role in *Caligula*, that play about the king who used to enjoy boiling people in pots just to hear them scream.

Bobby began to lose track of how many trips he was making out to the hall but somewhere around his fifth reconnoitring venture, he came face to face with Mr Hulka for the very first time. They weren't alone in the hall. There were two moving men who were rolling a long RCA television-stereo console between them. But Mr Hulka smiled and said hello. The voice that was so mellifluous sounded like a phony disc-jockey's. There was another overtone in Mr Hulka's voice. Even with that one word it was as if Bobby knew Hulka was telling him he was very aware of being observed, spied upon. They had only looked at each other for a moment and then Mr Hulka took off with the apes and the television, disappearing into 24G, and Bobby lingered in the incinerator room, tearing up an empty Macy's box that he had pleaded with his mother to let him throw out. He persisted in tearing the box into pieces, delaying as long as possible, shoving the pieces down the mouth revealed by the little metal

7

incinerator door. The door was hot so Bobby knew the fire was burning far below and he was glad it was such a very small door because it reminded him a little of the oven that the witch had in Hansel and Gretel when she tried to push the two kids into it. He did not ordinarily have macabre thoughts but there was something about the presence of Mr Hulka. It was as though he had an aura. Bobby had read a lot of articles about people giving off auras, these little vibrations emanating from them. It was as though his new neighbour's head had been anointed with a kind of evaporating oil, a slippery coating, which made Hulka's face shine like a gaudy bargain-basement souvenir. He looked almost religious, and yet if he was a saint he seemed like an artificial one, the kind of icon that would wear a headdress of cheap pinwheels and crepe paper streamers all flying outward. *The eyes are the mirror of the soul*, Bobby had been told a thousand times in his English class. And Mr Hulka's dark little beady eyes looked like he was filled with hate. It was the same old story with Mr Hulka's eyes as with anyone else's, Bobby decided. Those little balls of sight by which you could read a person's heart. Yes, Bobby told himself, he would have to get to know this one.

Chapter 2

Bobby couldn't wait to tell Lauri about Mr Hulka. Lauri
Geddes and her family had rented apartment 3A ever
since the Century Tower had started renting, which was
exactly thirteen months ago. The Geddes apartment was
of course much lower than Bobby's and overlooked the
outdoor swimming pool which made it a real nifty spot
to people-watch during the summer. Bobby and Lauri had
spent most of last August sitting on her terrace sipping
lemonade and ogling the motley group of tenants who
would make feeble attempts at socializing. They would see
adults rubbing lotions on their various extremities and
posing this way and that and clutching sun reflectors.
A lot of desperate secretaries seemed to be around in
bikinis throwing whammies to attract whatever unmarried
men there were. There was one woman who was so fat
that when she got in the pool she displaced about four
tons of water. And there were lots of mean little kids
running around shoving each other – brats trying to think
of all sorts of new ways to be aquatically cruel to each
other. Sometimes Bobby and Lauri would see a kid picking on someone else and Bobby would get up and stick
his two fingers into his mouth and let out a loud whistle
and say, 'Lay off you infantile nit or I'll come down there
and give you a knuckle sandwich.' In fact, Bobby and
Lauri had to appoint themselves as unofficial lifeguards
since the Century Tower's landlord was too cheap to have
a real lifeguard. He had spent a fortune putting up about
eighty-three 'swim-at-your-own-risk' signs, but that was it.
And here it was, the end of June, school all finished for
the year, and there was no question that Bobby and
Lauri would simply have to take up their posts on the
terrace of 3A as self-appointed *guardian angels* of the

subteen underdogs who would be fighting for their lives during the next two months in the overcrowded, under-sized swimming pool that absolutely reeked of chlorine.

'Angel' was a term that had to be applied somewhat loosely to Bobby now that he was fifteen years old and on semi-probation. Bobby's exterior was fairly successful. He was very good-looking with medium-length black hair and English-white skin and sound teeth and big green shining eyes. Even Bobby knew he was a class act. So he really didn't quite understand why he was sort of an outcast at school. He tried to explain it all to Lauri one infamous night when they became friends. And what he said that night was, 'The kids all react to me in the worst ways. The boys particularly. They think I'm an idiot and a professional jerk because I happen to hold poetry, good-ness and beauty above all other qualities. Everybody in Fort Lee High knows my name,' he told Lauri. 'They just don't like the way I talk out in class and believe that the world is a pretty terrific place and that kids don't all have to be berserk in order to get status points. I'm really a pacifist but so many kids yell things at me in the halls that sometimes I have to punch them a little.'

Lauri had had her own deep problems the first time they met so she had done only a lot of nodding in agree-ment, letting Bobby ramble on about every complaint he had in the world. 'They think I'm outspoken,' Bobby said. 'And it's just because I don't happen to like to sit around on the sidelines like they do, criticizing everybody else. I don't believe in tact. Maybe that's my problem. I mean, when I feel something I just say it. The reason I'm not accepted in our school is because I go against the grain, the grain of the kids, the teachers. They all don't like me. You'll find that out the longer you go there. They don't let me in the football team. They don't let me do any-thing. But I don't care. All I do is laugh. They can't hurt me. They don't hurt me at all.'

Lauri had nodded again and Bobby knew she didn't quite fall for the last line of his.

'Last year I was walking down the hall,' Bobby continued, 'and this one kid walked up to me and said, "You're Bobby Perkins, aren't you?" So I said, "Yes." And he said, "Well, I want you to know you're about the stupidest waste I've ever met." ' Bobby sighed. 'You know incidents like that have caused me to be aware of the inconsistencies of student behaviour.'

'Oh yes,' Lauri had agreed.

'They talk about being revolutionary,' Bobby began to sound off, 'but at the same time they're worried about whether the theme for the prom is going to be *Tropical Night* or *Springtime on a Star*. They talk about signing petitions to make those factories in Newark stop shoving sulphur dioxide into the air but what they are really worried about is if they're going to get their driver's licence next week. They talk about Communist suppression but what they're into is how to up their allowances.' Bobby had been able to tell by the expression on Lauri's face that she was really becoming impressed with him, so he decided to be even more effusive. 'If you hear any bitterness in my voice let me tell you it's purely intentional. I've been kicked around enough. There are too many flaws in people and society and particularly that school. They're not interested in what my ideas are. All those teachers care about is if I have the quotation marks and the exclamation points in the right place. And that's not what it's all about. They should listen to what I've got to say. They shouldn't try to kill off my imagination. Or anybody else's imagination! They're shoving all this stuff down our throats. We don't even know what it is. They should let our ideas out. Don't jump up and down on them, and write all those nasty little things with their red pens. I say only about twenty-five per cent of those teachers know what they're doing. I'm going to fix the ones that don't because one day I'm going to write a book and tell them how to really run a school so that you don't kill off the way a kid learns. Of course, I don't really know about other schools, but Fort Lee High as far as I'm concerned is a gigantic monument to man's attempt to educate his kids and his failure to do so. That's the way I feel about it. Kids have to learn by expressing themselves!'

Lauri had looked at him and finally had to try to balance the scales. 'A lot of teachers at Fort Lee High help me,' she said softly.

'Well, I told you there are some good ones. And besides, I'm just really sounding off right now. I'm really a very quiet person most of the time. I'm a nice kid except when somebody rubs me the wrong way and then I grab a megaphone and I start screaming into it, "I'm here, I'm here", and I'm always going to do that even if it makes people go deaf from my yelling!'

In truth, several of the teachers at Fort Lee High had picked Bobby out for his individuality during the first few weeks of his attendance there and he was punished accordingly. His first act of defiance was to refuse to go to study hall. He had told Miss Berkowitz, his grade adviser who happened to have only one arm, that study hall was simply a waste of time and a fill-in because of inept curricular planning by the staff to keep kids in school longer than they had to be. Besides, he pointed out, all the kids did in study hall was throw malted balls at poor Mr Kirchmorker when he wasn't looking, and Bobby didn't like that because Mr Kirchmorker was a wonderful civics teacher. He just happened to be a lousy disciplinarian. Then there was the time when Mr Kirchmorker got hit in the eye with a tangerine and Bobby got so angry at the kid who threw it that he socked the kid. But Bobby ended up being the one getting into trouble. He got ten demerits and he didn't even know what demerits were and he was hoping that maybe if he got enough of them they would try to give him the electric chair at a special assembly, but at the last minute before the switch was thrown he could shove the principal into the seat and fry him. Every week at the beginning there seemed to be some new crime Bobby got charged with. He refused to take gym third period because it got him all sweated up and the school had no shower facilities.

As it worked out, before the end of Bobby's first year at Fort Lee High his parents had been called in six times for conferences, and what most horrified the disciplinary staff of the school was that Bobby's parents openly expressed their love and belief in their son. Mr and Mrs Perkins had the nerve to say they thought their son was absolutely correct in most matters. Bobby Perkins was a kid who trusted his parents and they trusted him.

'Mr and Mrs Perkins,' the Dean of Boys had pronounced on one occasion, 'we can't have all the students running around saying whatever comes into their heads!'

'Why not?' Bobby's father enquired.

The Dean couldn't answer that one.

Then came the aforementioned infamous night.

It was a night when the school administration felt it had been completely vindicated because Bobby was finally apprehended by the police. The incident occurred at of all things an Italian block party right near the Century Tower Apartments – when four streets had been closed to traffic to allow local merchants to set up sausage and cookie stands and there were four rock bands to let the people musically jump up and down in the streets. The local bocce club set off fireworks on behalf of St Anthony, and wine, beer and lasagna seemed to ooze from everywhere. Bobby had gone to the block party alone and he was feeling very depressed as he strolled along the crowded streets watching the bursts of rockets in the sky reflect off the river and the silver webbing of the bridge. It was all so beautiful he almost forgot how alone he really was. Just before the infamy started he noticed Lauri Geddes at one stand. He had never spoken to her before but had seen her often moving through the lobby of the Century Tower or in the halls at Fort Lee High. She reminded him of a timid delicate angora cat. She was also alone and he could tell she was feeling very self-conscious because she was taking little bits out of her cannoli like a mouse

13

nibbling at cheese in a trap. Suddenly Bobby heard a gang of kids in a convertible hooting and honking their way as they broke through a barricade and began to invade the block party. The kids in the car were stoned and drunk, especially the driver who was at least two years older than Bobby, and Bobby was so ticked off at their nerve he just jumped right in front of the car forcing them to stop.

'Get out of the way,' the kid driving the car yelled — and then he made the mistake of throwing a beer can which hit Bobby on the head. Once again Bobby forgot his basically shy nature and jumped up on the hood and socked the driver. He got in a few good punches before the others started to really beat on him and by that time the police were on the scene. Everything would have worked out just fine if the kid Bobby had punched had not turned out to be the local police chief's son. As it was, Bobby was the only one who was dragged off to the police station, and once the police had him inside they threatened him with everything from reform school to a bop on the skull with a nightstick. Bobby began to feel as though he was back in school again, when there suddenly appeared a thin girl with long brown straight hair. She had been standing in the doorway and then stepped forward wiping some powdered sugar from her lips. She spoke in a very gentle but clear voice.

'He's innocent,' she said.

A silence flashed through the stationhouse. The three presiding officers turned to see where the voice had come from. Even the young bearded assistant cop to the right of the main desk stopped typing. The chief was a Sergeant Collins who looked like an irate Wizard of Oz, and he leaned forward from behind his towering desk, peering down with bulging eyes. Even the two Puerto Rican girls working behind the dusty glass of the computer report room peered out like bronzed goldfish sensing something strange was occurring to the customary choreography of the stationhouse. There was something more than a routine booking going on.

'Did you say something?' Sergeant Collins asked.

'He's innocent,' Lauri repeated. 'I was a witness.'

Bobby saw the girl's hands were trembling and he knew it had taken every drop of courage in her body to make her follow, come forward and bear witness for him. Nevertheless the police brayed illogically at them for the next twenty minutes. The kids just kept staring at each other as though in silent agreement that the world was for the most part unjust and often very noisy. The cops even worked up a phony call to the police commissioner and they announced that it was Bobby's luckiest day on earth that no charges were going to be pressed. But he would be on semi-probation. They kept yelling things like, 'What would your parents say?' and 'You should be thrown out of school!' But finally Bobby and Lauri were allowed to leave – and from that moment on Bobby Perkins and Lauri Geddes were as close as if they had signed a pact in blood.

Chapter 3

Lauri sat on one of the lounge chairs of her family's terrace. She kept looking back and forth from the pool just below to the pitcher of iced tea with two glasses on the small round white table next to her chair.

'Bobby's late,' her mother said, poking her head out the terrace door.

'I know,' Lauri said.

'He's usually so punctual,' Mrs Geddes reminded her, smiling, then pulled her head back and shut the glass door to seal the cool air inside. Lauri sat alone on the terrace but she wasn't worried. Bobby would be there soon enough. Something standardly berserk was probably happening, she thought. And at any moment he'd just come running in with some sort of report. She already expected it would have something to do with the new neighbour moving in next door to him. Half the building was talking about it. The doormen had already clued most people in that a Mr Hulka was moving into 24G. As it was, all arrivals had to plead and perform all sorts of acts of bribery with the staff in order to move into the Century Tower Apartments. One of the under-the-table deals was you had to cross the palm of the custodian with a little money to make sure the service elevators would be reserved for all the incoming furnishings. That sort of stuff never came in the front door. In fact there was a hierarchy of staff at the Century Tower that was staggering. You had doormen. There were concierges. There were lobby assistants, a garage manager, mailmen, parcel post deliverymen, window washers – paper delivery persons, daily paper delivery persons, Sunday paper delivery persons. There was an entire army of persons waiting to swoop down trying to snoop information and dig in like ticks for tips and especially to line up for big payoffs when Christmas came around. There were one or two nice guys working in the building. There was a man called Nick who was on the early shift as a lobby porter. He used to always show pictures of his grandchildren and he never had his hand out for a tip. He'd help with packages just because he wanted to help, and he had this wild dream about becoming a famous vocalist by re-recording 'The Talk of the Town'. Sometimes he'd just break out into song and start crooning away and Lauri and Bobby were the only ones who never made any fun of him. Everyone else working there was more like a blur to her. They all seemed to have phony faces and phony smiles. Lauri didn't think she could trust them as far as she could throw them. And there had been several robberies in the building already. Bobby had a theory that the main crook was a kid by the name of Rucci who was about eighteen and worked in the garage. Rucci's job was to sit in this little booth just inside, left of the garage doors, and he would press buttons that would make the garage doors open or close. Rucci could see cars arriving from his booth and he could see cars leaving. Rucci was also supposed to change bulbs but he never did. There were always light bulbs missing here or there and the whole garage was a very scary-looking place. It looked more suitable for growing mushrooms than parking Cadillacs and Continentals. Bobby also figured Rucci was the real one behind all the breaking and entering because he could really tell who was on vacation, and who was out and who was in, and all the other things you needed to know in order to rip off televisions and stereos or even jewellery and furs.

Rucci had such a twisted little sneaky face that Lauri once used to have fantasies that Rucci was going to kill her. She hated walking out of the front of the apartment house for she always thought he was going to come hopping out of his little glass cage and pull her into the garage and then press the button that would make that door come roaring down like a roller coaster and he'd do awful things to her. Of course, the problem with Lauri Geddes for over a year now had been that she thought everybody was out to kill her. Not only everybody, but everything. Objects as well. Bobby was the only one who knew what most of her fears were. In fact it had taken her a good two months to tell him all the ways she thought her life was in danger. That night she had saved him from being arrested at the police station she had told him a little bit about her phobia of death. She had tried to explain it wasn't a severe crippling kind of disposition. She was still able to walk out the door and it was only a part of her that was really afraid of dying. The other part of her really wanted to live. But she felt as though fate was really after her. She was even afraid to ride in cars because she thought they would turn over. She was afraid to go across bridges because she thought they were going to fall down. She was afraid to go in tunnels because she thought they were going to split in half. Also high on her list of fears were a fear of falling glass, a fear of falling aeroplanes, and a fear of falling cranes. She used to sit around waiting for earthquakes, tidal waves, sharks, encephalitis-carrying mosquitoes, and ballet dancers carrying sharp objects. There were times when she thought murderers were hiding in every shadow just waiting to get her. Careening buses and trucks were about to rush around every corner trying to crush her against a wall or smash through a store window to get at her. All the worst diseases in the world and poisons and flying saucers and black holes were collectively waiting to arrange her departure from this life. Every possible way of dying had crossed her mind. Bobby told her, 'Forget it, it's all in your head.' And when Bobby said that she believed it. She believed it every time she was with Bobby. But when she was alone she still thought the world was one big night-mare waiting to knock her off.

'What I'm most afraid of actually is that someone is going to grab me in the elevator and take me to the top of the building and throw me off,' she once told Bobby. That was last February and they had been drinking hot chocolate instead of iced tea in the Geddes apartment.

'I'd love to go that way,' Bobby remarked and then they had both burst into laughter. By this time they had known each other so well they couldn't wait to play the game because that's what it turned into. Lauri kept belly-aching how she was going to die by some new ghastly way, and Bobby would use psychology on her and say how terrific, that it was a brilliant way to go. He had discovered that was the best way to deal with her, and then they would both have a giggling fit and roll around on the floor. Of course, death wasn't the only thing they talked about. They loved talking about mischief and they loved school gossip and they must have gone to at least fifty movies – and they both were addicted to television and popcorn with double butter. But still death was lurking around, and Bobby knew very well, in fact they both knew very well, why the morbid game had come about. When you boiled it down, it really was a game in which Lauri Geddes kept complaining that her death was imminent and Bobby Perkins kept complaining that his death wasn't. Lauri knew whenever Bobby said how beautiful it would be to die that he was really only covering the hurt, tending to the scars that had been left on his ego by all the kids at school who hated him for being the wonderful individualist he really was. Lauri knew he didn't really mean that he wanted to die and the one thing she was sure of was that no matter what restrictions society and school tried to put on Bobby, he'd put up one grand fight against them, right down the line. And that was what she loved most about him. In fact, she was very deeply in love with him, but she hadn't the faintest idea of how to move their friendship into a more romantic arena. Besides, even though it had been almost a year now, Lauri was still recovering from something that had happened in her old neighbourhood. She was just fourteen years old when she had seen what had happened to her neighbours in Edison. At that time, Lauri was living in a development – one split-level ranch right next to the other – and it was the middle of the night. There were sounds, screams, someone banging on the door of the Geddeses' house. It was the Kaminsky boy who lived next door. He had been drunk; he had come home in the middle of the night and tried to cook a steak but the grease had caught fire. By the time Lauri and her parents were out on the lawn the Kaminsky boy had run back into the house and the house was bubbling with smoke. The kitchen fire had spread. Lauri's father and some of the other men from the neighbourhood had tried to get in the doors but great fingers of flame had pushed them back. The Kaminsky family was trapped in the upstairs and someone had a flashlight. Lauri would never forget the flickering of that light behind the window shades, the silhouettes moving with panic from one room to another. Finally the light and the screams had disappeared and the house and the entire family were lost before the fire engines had even arrived.

And that was why the Geddes family now lived in apartment 3A at the Century Tower. Her folks decided she needed a change of scene in order to try to forget the unforgettable. They had sold their house in Edison and thought Lauri might lose her fright, her nightmares, in the busy comings and goings of a high rise.

The terrace door opened and Lauri's mother peeked out again.

'Bobby's on the phone,' Mrs Geddes said with great relief.

'Thanks, Mom,' Lauri replied, jumping up and dashing inside. She had a feeling their usual afternoon salon was going to move to a higher altitude. Her mother handed her the phone and gave her a wink.

Lauri blushed, took the receiver and put it to her ear. 'Hello,' she said.

'You have to get up here right away,' Bobby's voice commanded.

'I can't,' Lauri stated. 'Besides, I've got all the tea set up down here – and also I had a dream that if I got in an elevator the thing would fall today.'

'Don't worry about it,' Bobby ordered. 'Just get in and press button number twenty-four. Then close your eyes.'

'All right,' Lauri agreed. 'I'm coming.' She hung up, but inside it really wasn't all right. She was really afraid that thing *was* going to fall. It was unnatural for people to get in these big metal boxes with cables attached to them that would go flying up and down in the air. Oh sure, there were these little cards that inspectors made believe they signed saying that everything was okay. But she didn't believe that. She knew human nature and part of being human was being lazy and she was positive they didn't check everything that should be checked. But it was always the same. After she went through every possible thing that could go wrong, there was one pervading thought which was that Bobby would be at the end of the journey waiting for her. And that always gave her enough strength to get into any kind of contraption. Whenever she thought of Bobby, it gave her courage.

Chapter 4

Bobby had left the door to his apartment ajar with the screwdriver his father usually kept on top of the stereo cabinet. Bobby himself was out on the terrace with his face squashed between the terrace partition and the brick of the building, and he didn't want to have to get up to answer the door when Lauri arrived. When she did get there she was carrying the iced-tea pitcher, and the ice cubes were clinking back and forth against its sides. He signalled her to ditch the pitcher and get out on the terrace. He also included a finger to his lips that she should join him silently.

Lauri gently placed the pitcher down on the Perkinses' kitchen table, tiptoed across the living-room, and came out the terrace door. Bobby motioned her to the partition.

'Get a load of this,' Bobby whispered.

Lauri put her left eye to the edge of the big plastic rectangle. At first all she noticed was the empty terrace of the apartment next door, apartment 24G. Then she realized if she squeezed her head real hard and bent slightly she could see a good portion of the 24G living-room. And there she managed to focus on a full-grown man who was busy at work setting up a dolls' house. Specifically he was arranging a set of tiny chairs around a miniature dinette table.

'That's Mr Hulka,' Bobby wheezed.

Lauri noted the dolls' house was one of the largest ones she had ever seen. It was like a Colonial mansion that looked a little like a wedding cake. In fact it was so fascinating she made the mistake of leaning too hard against the partition and it made a *twang* that caused Mr Hulka to turn and look towards his terrace. Lauri got a look at his eyes and bolted backwards, stepping on

Bobby's feet. He let out a cry of pain and in an instant the two of them were dashing inside, slamming the terrace door behind them. They fled into the kitchen where they couldn't be seen even if Mr Hulka wanted to come out on *his* terrace and peer around the outside of the mutual partition.

'Is this what you made me take an elevator for?' Lauri asked.

'Yeah, it's some dolls' house, isn't it?' Bobby said, plopping himself down at the kitchen table. 'And that's not all. There's a lot of weird things in that apartment. I mean, really weird things. Pour us a shot of tea, will you?' he added.

Lauri got two glasses out of the kitchen cabinet. She had helped Mrs Perkins fix dinner so many times she knew where everything was, or at least was *supposed* to be.

'Why is your hand shaking?' Bobby wanted to know as he watched her pouring the tea.

'My hand is not shaking.'

'What do you mean it's not shaking?'

'*It's not shaking.*'

'Of course it's shaking. You got a good look at him, didn't you?' Bobby wanted to know.

'What do you mean I got a *good* look at him?'

'You know very well what I mean.'

'No, I didn't,' Lauri said, not wanting to remember the pair of fierce-looking corneas that had spun around from the dolls' house. Those eyes reminded her of something she had once read in a magazine about a famous male movie star. There was this man who used to play gangster roles and they said the secret of his success was that he had the eyes of a woman and the face of an animal. She'd always remembered that description but in this case it was as though Mr Hulka was the reverse. He seemed to have the eyes of an animal and the face of a woman. Not exactly a woman but there was something androgynous about the face, like a Russian lady wrestler.

'He seems very nice,' Lauri decided to fib. 'And it's very

nice for a father to set up a dolls' house for his kids.'

'He doesn't have any kids.'

'Who says?'

'I checked downstairs with Miss Lawton, the renting agent. You know what a big mouth she has. All Mr Hulka has is a wife and as far as I've been able to keep track, *three* dolls' houses.'

'Nobody's perfect,' Lauri quipped, and they both had a good laugh.

Then the rest of the afternoon they hardly spoke about Mr Hulka at all. There were too many other important possibilities for the summer coming up. And before long they were into their favourite pastime – which was looking off the terrace and over the terrain of their past exploits. The things they had done on the Palisade Cliffs and the George Washington Bridge – and then across the way on the New York side of the river where The Cloisters was set on top of the hills above the Henry Hudson Parkway. At least a couple of times a week they looked off the terrace and reminisced about the time they borrowed choir robes from Grace Methodist Church and got dressed as a monk and a nun. Lauri had spent three days making the hat which looked a little bit like a giant dove sitting on her head. And they had gone up to the grounds of The Cloisters which was a religious museum that housed the intricate Unicorn tapestries. Bobby had added a hood to his robe so he really looked monastic. And Lauri had also fashioned a stiff white bib, and they strolled The Cloisters grounds all day sipping Coca-Colas and speaking loudly so the tourists could hear them. They kept saying that they were appointed by the archdiocese to guard the Unicorn because of their chosen spiritual identification with all things mystical and magical. Another time, right on the edge of the cliffs, they had held a marshmallow roast which the Fort Lee police had raided and made them extinguish. Bobby had told them he was the son of the Rockefellers who owned all the land but they had chased them away anyway. It seemed like Fort Lee had only about three or four policemen who worked the cliff areas and in less than a year Bobby and Lauri had got to know all of them through their high jinks. The one who usually caught them was Patrolman Petrie. Patrolman Petrie was also the one who came after them on the middle of the George Washington Bridge the day Lauri and Bobby decided to walk across wearing ape masks. Some of the cars did start to swerve and Lauri thought it might be a little bit dangerous but in the end she really did think the police made much too much fuss about the whole event. After all, there was no law against walking across a bridge with ape masks on.

'There's no such *specific* law on the books,' Bobby had said. And the cops just sort of scratched their heads and drove them off the bridge.

'You two just like to get everybody's goat, don't you?' Patrolman Petrie had observed.

Of course the worst thing Bobby and Lauri ever did they never really got caught at and that was throwing balloons filled with water off Bobby's terrace. They did that almost all of April and it was a lot of fun watching the big rubber balls tumble twenty-four floors and then splash near Rucci sitting at the garage cage. One exploded right in front, splashing the glass in front of him. One time they threw a water balloon too far to the right and it landed right in the middle of some people who were on their way home from a wedding. That was the same evening Bobby and Lauri had their very profound discussion about how Lauri thought that Bobby was really a reincarnation of Jack in 'Jack and the Beanstalk'. And Bobby had decided after a lot of thought that he thought Lauri was the Sleeping Beauty. They both had no trouble finding out this information because all they had to do was ask each other what their favourite childhood story was. Bobby always thought of himself as Jack, the devilish lazy kid who would trade the family cow any day for a pack of magical beans and when the vine grew he knew he'd be the first to climb it, especially knowing there was a giant waiting to do battle when he reached the top. The only thing was that Bobby didn't plan on being knocked off; he figured he would knock off the giant. Bobby could just see the headline in the Fort Lee newspaper if he ever did that. BOBBY PERKINS DEFEATS BIG GUY IN THE SKY. Lauri had literally fallen out of her terrace chair when Bobby had come up with that line. He always loved to think of headlines but when they got around to her as Sleeping Beauty she became more pensive. She knew, like Sleeping Beauty, she didn't really want to die at all. Inside her, part of her felt like a young princess, especially when she was with Bobby. Nevertheless, Lauri did feel an evil curse was put on her by a witch. The witch of Edison, New Jersey. And when she reached a certain age she would stick herself with some kind of needle and fall dead. There would be no commutation of her curse to sleep for a hundred years, though, she felt. Unless of course someone *did* come along and give her a last-minute gift of life. That was the way the story went. Sometimes in the middle of the night Lauri would actually wake up from a nightmare where she knew no one was going to save her. The real Sleeping Beauty had awoken only when a prince came along and gave her a kiss, and she just felt sure that Bobby was never really going to like her the way she wanted him to. She sort of accepted that and she'd make up these letters sometimes in daydreams. She'd say, *Dear Bobby, I understand that we can only be buddies and I really feel terrible about that but I accept it all and so I'm going to die anyway but promise me, Bobby, that when I do die you won't let them cremate me, okay? Because I don't like fire.*

Lauri was about to get into all those mystical elements again as she poured the last of the iced tea that afternoon. But suddenly the sound of a hammer tapping reached her ears.

'Hulka's probably installing a Baby Grand in the dolls' house,' Bobby said. But he didn't laugh, and neither did Lauri. They just listened and wondered, and remembered those *eyes*.

Chapter 5

Bobby had to wait almost a week before he got his first look at Mrs Hulka. The occasion was rather spectacular. Tuesday night, when the buzzer of the Perkinses' apartment sounded simultaneously with a banging on the door, Bobby's father ran and opened it and there was Mr Hulka, looking like a red-faced gorilla. Just behind him was his wife, a very plastic-looking woman, tall, thin, and with a head of very carefully coiffured, bleached blonde hair. Mrs Hulka looked like the kind of dummy you would see in a fancy department-store window.

'I have to use your terrace,' Mr Hulka yelled as he just barged right by Bobby's mother and father. He literally ran across the living-room, threw open the doors to the Perkinses' terrace, nearly breaking them, and then swung dangerously around the plastic partition so that he landed on his own terrace. Bobby and his folks just stood frozen, except for their heads, which swung from one direction to the other direction as though watching a tennis match. At their door stood Mrs Hulka with her phony hair looking as if it was popping out of her rich, black silk coat, and at the terrace was just the gaping hole of the open door where Mr Hulka had disappeared like a boomerang bat. Mrs Hulka had cranky, large blue eyes, flickering under a weight of mascara, which made her look like she was auditioning for the part of a movie extravaganza version of Cleopatra. Everybody was making guttural sounds as though trying to think of what to say, but then there came a sound from the hallway as Mr Hulka pulled open the door to his apartment and jumped back out in the hall to stand next to his wife. He had done a complete circle, right through the Perkinses' house, out on to the Perkinses' terrace, then on to his own terrace, through his living-room and back out into the hall.

'I thought there were burglars trying to rip off the place,' Mr Hulka explained. 'My key wouldn't fit in and I found *this*.' He held forth a small piece of metal that he claimed had been jammed into the keylock. 'That's an old trick of crooks so they have some warning before the owners of an apartment can open up their door and come in.'

'Are you sure no one's still hiding inside?' Mr Perkins asked.

'I'm sure,' Mr Hulka said. 'They probably kept their eye on the elevator and saw I was coming up to the floor. They cleared out before they even got started.'

Mrs Perkins cleared her throat. 'They could be in a closet or behind a shower curtain.'

'They never got in,' Mr Hulka assured. 'I have enough locks on our door to require dynamite to blast them off. Sorry to interrupt,' he added abruptly, and then propelled his wife swiftly into their own apartment, slamming the door behind them.

Bobby's father closed his door and leaned against it. He looked mildly puzzled and remarked, 'How weird.'

'So many rich people are weird,' Mrs Perkins observed, going on with her business, which at that moment was creating an acrylic collage. She had been at a particularly thrilling moment, learning how to stick tissue paper on to a canvas and letting ink stain its way into artistic shapes. 'Gravity paints better than I do,' she muttered, and then had an afterthought. 'You know, perhaps I should have offered the Hulkas some coffee,' she said. 'I mean, they didn't formally introduce themselves to us, but I mean if someone has run through your apartment and jumped around your terrace partition, I guess you know them well enough to offer them a little beverage.'

'Real peculiar,' Mr Perkins said, returning his attention to his tool chest and the stereo cabinet. Bobby used to love the way his father had to constantly make new adjustments on the massive equipment that hung off the whole slab of wall right next to the main entrance. It was located to create perfect acoustical aesthetics and Bobby liked the idea that his father made everything serviceable. The fact that most people kept their stereos in the living-room wasn't important.

Bobby figured the Hulkas were probably thinking how peculiar the Perkinses were, since it probably didn't take them long to size up that the Perkins digs weren't exactly straight out of *Good Housekeeping*. Bobby himself was very proud that his parents weren't the least bit ashamed that their apartment was a creative environment. Since Bobby was four years old he had looked upon his father as an unrecognized gifted mathematician who deserved much more than his company ever paid him. As it was, they still sent him to lots of glamorous places like Ohio and Maryland when they needed to supply a computer troubleshooter. The fact that Mr Perkins looked a little dishevelled and motley like their furniture was probably the only reason, Bobby decided, that his father never got very high up the corporate ladder of success. If he wore fancy handkerchiefs like Mr Hulka, they'd probably be living next door in a big G apartment themselves. Most of the junk in the Perkinses' place was left over from the days Mr Perkins really tried to make a living as an inventor, and Bobby was conceited about the fact that his father was the first one to create a talking wristwatch, which was a blessing to blind people, because no matter where they were, all they had to do was press a little button on the side and a taped voice would say, 'It's twelve twenty-five,' or whatever the time really was. If three people hadn't invented talking wristwatches that same year and beat Mr Perkins to the patent, Bobby knew they'd really be rolling in money now. Then his mother could have had all the room she needed for her multi-media art products. He really felt his mother was a great lady and the fact that she had failed at watercolours, oils, ceramics, plywood, tin, brass, clay, blowtorch, etchings, ink emulsions and practically every known material and technique of artistic expression known to man didn't diminish his admiration for her in the least. What Bobby adored most about his folks was that they weren't limited to intellectual life but that they combined it with mountain climbing and camping. Sometimes his mother and father would go away for a couple of weeks straight, which is why the Perkinses were the only family at the Century Tower who had a station-wagon with an eight-foot Styrofoam camping module on its roof. Mr Perkins had invented the outsized module the year that several other people had already beat him to *that* patent. His father was never bitter about it. He was always hopeful about the future. He could recover quickly – like he was already singing, working with a screwdriver, attaching new wires, rearranging units of the stereo as though Mr Hulka had never invaded just a few minutes before. Bobby also appreciated the fact that he didn't have to go with them when they went camping. He used to go a lot when he was younger, but it got a little boring after a while, climbing Whiteface Mountain and visiting Santa's Workshop. Now that Bobby was getting older he found it harder and harder to keep up with his parents. It seemed like they could climb mountains faster and he'd be dragging along and they'd have to be calling, 'Come on, Bobby! You can do it! You can do it!' That was the one flaw about his parents, Bobby decided. They were just too active. Actually, one of the reasons he still liked to go along once in a while was they always let him drive the car. He used to be able to zip that station-wagon up the Palisades Parkway, fly west to pick up the Thruway, and then really just set that car right on the road and head for the Adirondacks. And when it came to scooting around curves in the mountains, there was nobody better than he was. Of course, he had been driving since he was ten years old. His father used to let him drive around empty supermarket lots on Sundays. But now that Lauri had come into his life, driving for its own sake had lost some of its sparkle. Maybe if he could get his hands on a Ferrari, or a Corvette, something a little different and with a little extra zip, he'd like it better. And his folks respected him for admitting that he didn't want to go along. They knew how he felt about Lauri, and they knew because of Lauri's background that she needed him more than they did. They seemed to be really able to understand that two kids can need each other and be trusted and have more things on their brains than to smoke pot all the time or organize orgies. The very best thing he liked about his parents was any time they *did* take off they didn't give him a big lecture on do's and don't's. All they would do was give him a great big hug and say, 'Watch out for the milkman.' He never even knew what the expression meant, but he figured it was sort of old-timers' expression to keep clear of anyone evil.

Bright and early the next morning, after the Hulka burglary scare, Bobby shot right down to tell Lauri all about it. They took up their lounging positions on Lauri's terrace and looked down at the pool. There was nobody in it yet but the chlorine odour had no trouble scaling the three floors to their nostrils. Bobby talked a mile a minute about how there was no question in his mind after seeing Mr Hulka's gymnastic abilities and the way he was able to deduce things that he was either an FBI agent or with the CIA.

'You should have seen him,' Bobby babbled on. 'It was incredible the way he just swung around there, knew all about jamming pieces of metal into locks. Anybody else who would have come across a piece of metal jammed in their lock probably would have just gone running back down the hall yelling, "Help, police! Help, police!"'

Bobby took a sip of the pineapple juice Lauri had mixed for them. 'And *she* looked like a high-class Barbie doll, that Mrs Hulka,' Bobby added.

Lauri let out a sigh. She knew what Bobby would be saying at any moment. He would say what he always said when someone tantalizingly new moved into the Century Tower.

'I don't know about you,' Bobby finally infiltrated, 'but I think we ought to get our Welcome Wagon warmed up again, don't you?'

'No, I don't,' Lauri said quickly. But then she smiled. The last time they got their Welcome Wagon going was when the Jacksons moved into 14A, with their Advent television, and Bobby wanted to see *Star Trek* on the giant screen. Then there was the time when they had heard that 17H, the Goldbergs, had installed their own Jacuzzi. That got the Welcome Wagon going so they could get a look at that. And only once did Lauri want the Welcome Wagon, and that was when she had seen the incredible drapes that 7H had put up. They were scalloped and looked like they were worth thousands of dollars.

Most of the whole next week Bobby tried to keep track of the Hulkas. He wanted to get a feel for their comings and goings, because one of the hardest parts of conducting a Welcome Wagon visit was to make sure that the people you were welcoming were home when you got there. This aspect was even more difficult than Bobby had imagined because the Hulkas had three cars. They had a yellow Volkswagen, which Mrs Hulka seemed to use mainly for shopping. Then they had a green Eldorado with a white vinyl roof, which apparently was used when both of them went out on these great big fancy evening dates, probably to the opera or the ballet. And then they had a long black Chevrolet station-wagon with these strangely dark tinted windows. Even worse was they kept the Volkswagen on the first level of the garage. Then they had the Eldorado in a space on level two. And for some reason they had the station-wagon stuck far down on level three. Bobby felt like he was running around in labyrinths, going up and down the elevators to all three different levels of the garage. What he really didn't like was that he would have to come back and forth in front of TV cameras that he knew connected straight to Rucci's booth at the garage exit. There's one thing he didn't need, having that teenage crook knowing his comings and goings. He knew Rucci probably lined up only the expensive apartments, but he still wouldn't trust him if Rucci happened to take a shine to one of his own jackets or sweaters. But throughout all this reconnoitring, one thing seemed obvious to Bobby and that was that Mr Hulka seemed to prefer using the station-wagon at rather strange hours. On Wednesday of the first week, Bobby had trouble sleeping and got up around three o'clock in the morning and happened to look off his terrace and saw Mr Hulka's station-wagon roaring out of the garage like the Batmobile. Another time when he had trouble sleeping, he heard the Hulkas' front door slam. So he went out on the terrace again, and sure enough, after a few minutes the station-wagon came flying out again. Bobby was usually able to keep track of it for several blocks, but after that, even though he was on the twenty-fourth floor, there were too many trees lining the blocks below and if the car didn't disappear out of sight there, it certainly got lost behind the buildings of the town. Once it went straight across the bridge and Bobby was able to follow it when it turned and went south on the Henry Hudson Parkway. It got off down the river at 125th Street and then disappeared. But Bobby looked upon all this stuff as sort of information gathering. His favourite teacher at school was a chemistry teacher who taught him how to apply scientific procedures to real life. The procedure he really found useful was to *define the problem, consider all the causes of the problem, then list the possible solutions* and ultimately *figure out the best solution*. After enough days of research he finally submitted his report to Lauri. The Hulkas were always home on Sunday evening.

Lauri accepted the information and then got her side of the plot in motion. On the Saturday morning before they were going to have the Welcome Wagon ready, Lauri broke the news to her mother.

'Bobby and I want to visit the Hulkas who just moved into twenty-four-G,' Lauri said straight out. That was all she ever had to say because, as usual, Mrs Geddes sprang into action, saying how thoughtful it was that once more Lauri and Bobby were going to welcome another new family. Mrs Geddes helped her daughter plan all the kinds of food they wanted to bring. She suggested a Pyrex platter of spaghetti and meatballs and a pot of pork sausages, just like they had brought to the family with the Advent television set. 'Or maybe you'd rather have a platter of veal parmigiana,' Mrs Geddes enquired. 'That tastes better the second day.'

'I think they'd like a cassata cake,' Lauri suggested.

'Oh, that's a good idea,' Mrs Geddes agreed. 'And some cookies, with chocolate sprinkles on them.'

The excitement in her mother's eyes made Lauri want to just give her a big squeeze and tell her she was just the best mother in the whole world. Lauri knew if she did that her mother would just start crying because they both knew what was really going on underneath. Her mother's voice always sounded on the verge of tears anyway, whenever it seemed that Lauri was taking another step forward to get out in the world. Anything that Lauri and Bobby wanted to do was okay with Mrs Geddes, anything that would take her daughter's mind off of that terrible, terrible thing that had happened in Edison. 'That Bobby's a doll,' Mrs Geddes would say twenty times a day. 'That Bobby's a doll.' She said that all through the cooking preparations. She said it all through the shopping for the meats and at the butcher's and at the supermarket. 'That Bobby is really a doll.'

'He's very nice to me,' Lauri agreed. 'I guess we like each other.'

'Like each other,' Mrs Geddes pushed. 'He adores you. That boy's a saint and he loves you.'

'I wouldn't go that far,' Lauri said.

'What do you mean?' Mrs Geddes sounded offended. 'He worships you. I'm so proud of the way he's made you not afraid to go through the Lincoln Tunnel any more. It makes it so much easier to get you to Gimbels.'

Lauri helped her mother cook, and when her father got

home from his job as a quality control worker at the Hoboken Smelting Works, he knew the minute he walked in the door what was up. He insisted on contributing a bottle of Asti spumante. 'I mean, it's a G-line apartment, isn't it?' he reminded everyone. 'I mean, this has got to be a classy apartment. We don't want them to think we just got off the boat.' Then he grabbed his evening newspaper and sat in the living-room, listening to the banging of the veal and the aroma of bubbling tomato sauce floating its way out from the kitchen. One time he looked in to check on how things were going.

'Test the sausage,' Mrs Geddes said seductively.

'You bet,' Mr Geddes said, grabbing a piece in his fingers and munching on it.

Mrs Geddes waited anxiously for a reaction.

A big smile grew across Mr Geddes's face and he put his arm around his wife. 'You're the best cook in the world.'

Lauri watched them and thought wouldn't it be nice if Bobby said that to her one day when they were married and living happily ever after. In fact, the little scene between her mother and father had set her off into one of her daydreaming letter-writing exercises – another letter she would love to send to Bobby to tell him all the things she was feeling inside. There were little things she was starting to feel besides worrying about whether a Mack truck was going to knock her down. As she stirred the spaghetti sauce, she began to wish she had enough nerve to write something like, *Dear Bobby, baby Jesus, do I miss you, even now as I'm stirring this succulent, savoury sauce. I have so many paragraphs to write you in my mind, but I'm so afraid of assuming things I have no right to assume about us. But I have lots of dreams and you're always in them. Sometimes I think of myself as a student and you're a famous writer and you're teaching me everything I know. I love the headlines you write. You really have a way with words and ideas, and you know, Bobby, what I'd really like to have from you is a picture* of yourself so that even when you weren't next to me I could just look at it all the time. Maybe we could go into one of those machines where they take four snapshots and you'd let me have them and I'd keep them right next to my bed so I wouldn't have to miss you, even though I know you're only twenty-one floors higher than me in the same building. Sometimes I lie awake all night thinking of you sleeping high above me in the air. Sometimes I think of us doing very physical things together because we really feel for each other and want to be as close together as we possibly can. I want to know so many things, like did you ever have a girl-friend, I mean, a real girl-friend, not just a buddy like me. I had a dream about you once that you were in love with a girl who was in charge of the clock in the tower of a large municipal building. Isn't that strange? And sometimes I have the feeling that in some ways you are just as uptight and afraid as I am. Maybe I'm even selfish. I don't think you're selfish, Bobby, and maybe we both have some problems about being able to show love to each other, real love. Every time I think of love my dream begins to go up in flames and I have a mental block. I can't even watch my father light a match without remembering things I don't want to remember. Bobby, every night I say my prayers and hope I turn into a very lovely girl, that I'm smart and modern enough for you and I want us to have two kids. This humble student needs you — a great writer of great headlines. I feel so warm and alive when I think of you and yet sometimes I get very frightened because I don't know the ending. I know the middle of my dreams. Sometimes I even know the beginnings — but I don't know if I'm sure that you'll ever really care for me as a lover should. I'm so frightened about the end of our journey, but I have to stop this daydreaming now because I have to add some oregano. You can only add oregano to a spaghetti sauce at the end or its delicate flavour will singe and disappear.

Chapter 6

By the time Sunday night actually came around, Bobby was practically exhausted from all the pre-planning that had to go into the visit to the Hulkas. It had seemed like a good enough idea for a while but all that work sort of put a damper on things. Besides, his report card had arrived and he had failed everything – especially English. He always wrote on crazy topics like *My Favourite Sleeping Room* and *Wake Up And Live* or *Tomorrow You May Meet a Neutron Bomb*. All his compositions came back with the teacher's comments on them. They all said 'Magnificent', 'What an imagination', 'What rotten grammar!'. That was all very nice, but Bobby never had the heart to confess that almost everything he wrote was documentary, not fiction, not really fiction. Every story was based on reality, and that included the time he thought he once saw a leprechaun near Radio City Music Hall. Granted he had just been to a dentist who had given him some nitrous oxide gas in order to yank out a tooth, but he was positive he had seen a little gnomelike creature darting along the edge of a fountain of an office building, singing, 'One potato, two potato, three potato, four.' He felt a little badly about the report card and he could just see the headlines in all the newspapers if he had really put a great deal of importance on academic achievement: BOARD OF ED DRIVES ANOTHER KID TO SUICIDE. But most of his energy these days was being devoted to rehabilitating Lauri. He decided that that was one girl who needed someone to look after her and that God or Nature or some strange force had appointed him to assure her that life was really worth living, even though it looked boring and dangerous and horrible at first inspection. And that was the thing he really liked about the latest Welcome

Wagon caper when he really thought the matter out. Whenever they were involved in a plan, some terrific activity, he noticed Lauri didn't fret so much about being demolished in some rare cataclysmic event. Whenever Bobby would plan an adventure she would seem to take it on like a script and behave like an enthusiastic, somewhat nervous ingénue, absorbed in all the details. This whole technique Bobby had devised to help Lauri seemed to be a lot of little shows because he felt that Lauri was like some of the movie stars he had seen on the late-night talk shows, where some actress would come out and talk like an idiot while she was being interviewed, but then she'd suddenly leap to life as she was called upon to recite a poem or do a scene. Lauri just needed scripts, too, he decided, but they were getting harder and harder to come by. After all, Mr and Mrs Hulka weren't exactly the most exciting item he could think of. He often wondered why actors and actresses seemed to be such boobs when they weren't in a play or a movie or a two-hour TV special. He decided that was mostly because the whole world seemed to be in show business in one way or another, everybody doing anything for attention, climbing up the sides of buildings or blowing people's heads off. Of course, he never stressed the violent part of the news when telling Lauri, but he was quite aware of it. The world was so freaky, he felt. Really very freaky indeed and no one was doing much about it. But he was going to try. He was going to try no matter what names kids called him in the halls. No matter how crazy he seemed he still wasn't quite ready to give up on the world. There must be some way to save it in spite of all the really *awful* politicians and executives and people doing everything on earth to cheat and store up their own little kingdoms here on earth.

At a quarter to six that evening Bobby ran a last-minute check at each of the garage levels to make sure all the Hulkas' cars were in their assigned spots. Even Rucci was in his booth and Bobby could see that he was reading a comic book as usual, instead of keeping his eyes on the television screens so he could see who was trying to break in and out of the building via the garage. A few minutes before six Bobby arrived at Lauri's apartment. Mr and Mrs Geddes set them up with all the culinary offerings and pushed them out the door with so much gaiety, he had the strangest feeling that Lauri and he were sailing on the *Leonardo da Vinci* out of Naples. He had to admit the veal looked absolutely delicious and the cassata cake was certainly moist enough. Most of all, he was impressed by the big yellow sign Mr Geddes had created, which declared, WELCOME MR AND MRS HULKA. He hung it around Bobby's neck.

Bobby carried the veal and the bottle of Asti spumante which had been wrapped in foil so that it twisted at its neck into a great flower formation. Lauri's attention had to be undivided on balancing the cake, so she didn't even think about getting into the elevator until after the doors had closed and it had started hurtling upward.

'A really terrific job,' Bobby said.

'That's nice of you to say so.' Lauri nodded. 'We try,' she added with a wink. 'We try.'

They stumbled out of the elevator. Bobby had to hold his back against the door which kept trying to close and squash Lauri with the cake. Eventually they were safely in the hall, and the doors had closed and they began to hobble down the long pathway which stopped smack at the Hulkas' door. Immediately to the right was the door of the Perkinses' apartment and Bobby was tempted to ring that one first so his mother and father could get a gander at their sumptuous culinary burden. As it was he was lucky enough to press the buzzer of the Hulka apartment without dropping anything.

It was Mr Hulka who opened the door. He looked quite surprised for a moment, Bobby thought, and more informal than usual. This time he had no tie or jacket, just a chequered shirt and dark slacks. He looked more normal – even his eyes looked less extreme. Then Bobby noticed the martini glass in his left hand and decided that was probably the explanation.

'Hello,' Mr Hulka said, his surprise changing into a big smile.

'Welcome to Century Tower,' Bobby said authoritatively.

'Well, I'll be!' Mr Hulka exclaimed, looking at the big sign hanging from Bobby's neck. Without a moment's hesitation, almost as though he had been waiting for them, he spun around and called out, 'Veronica, Veronica. We've got visitors!'

In a flash Mr Hulka had practically pushed Bobby and Lauri into the apartment and had the door closed behind them. Mrs Hulka was sweeping grandly towards them, talking a mile a minute with a martini glass in her left hand. Bobby hardly understood a word she was saying.

'I'm Robert Perkins,' Bobby said. 'And this is Miss Lauri Geddes. We're official representatives of the Welcome Wagon and we want you to know that it behoves us greatly that you decided to take residence at this garden spot of Fort Lee.'

'Yes,' Lauri said, proffering forth the cassata cake to Mrs Hulka, who had to set her drink down before she could grasp it.

'Why, this is lovely,' Mrs Hulka said, stumbling towards a sideboard and plopping the cake down on it. She then shot like a shark to get her martini glass and lead Lauri and Bobby in towards the living-room.

'Yep,' Bobby said for no particular reason, and he pushed the platter of veal parmigiana into Mr Hulka's right hand, which was large enough to hold a basketball.

'Come in, come in,' Mr Hulka kept repeating, still smiling like he had just got the punch line to a joke. Bobby stuck the bottle of Asti spumante on the sideboard next to the cassata cake and then began to fumble his way farther into the Hulkas' domain. It was all very confusing with everyone talking at the same time. Platters being handed this way and that. Bobby had never heard

so much small talk in his life. It seemed like a series of
non sequiturs, and a bit like a French comedy with plates
being moved from here to there and bottles going this way
and that. The cassata cake must have been admired about
four times, and then someone knocked over the bottle of
Asti spumante, but it didn't break because it bounced on
a purple carpet that must have been about three inches
thick. Bobby had wanted to seem suave but when the
bottle fell he jumped down on the throw rug like he was
a dog retrieving a bone. The purple was so bright it
practically blinded him, and when he stood up and put
the bottle back on the sideboard he kept rubbing his eyes
to try to get rid of the invasion of colour. Mrs Hulka was
doing an excessive amount of spinning to show off her
fancy golden bathrobe which was trimmed at the sleeves
with swirls of light feathers. Finally all the props seemed
to have made their way into their various spots, and
Bobby and Lauri had been seated on a gorgeous sofa
flanked by cheap Mexican elephant end tables. Bobby
was so proud of Lauri because he thought she was acting
extraordinarily sophisticated, and Mr and Mrs Hulka kept
doing all the talking, all the time referring to themselves
as Jack and Veronica, Veronica and Jack. It was Veronica
this and Jack that. It was not Mr and Mrs Hulka. It was
now just Jack and Veronica, and Veronica and Jack, *and
Bobby and Lauri*; they were all first-naming each other.
All Mr and Mrs Hulka kept doing was praising the cutlets
and cake as though they were items of sacrifice. Bobby
was dumbfounded because he never once had been in the
presence of two people who had obviously needed a
Welcome Wagon more than Mr and Mrs Hulka. The
other times they had pulled the Welcome Wagon stunt
on other families they had had pleasant receptions but
nothing like this. Of course, he was certain Mr and Mrs
Hulka were half loaded and when he and Lauri were asked
what they wanted to drink, Bobby blurted out, 'Martinis
will be fine, thank you.' Lauri's eyes widened to the size
of overcoat buttons. 'I'll take a Coca-Cola, if you don't

42

mind, thank you.'

The Hulkas laughed even louder and from that moment on Bobby decided the whole session was turning into nothing but a gathering of socialites of equal status shooting the breeze. They compared apartment numbers, and Mr Hulka was just amazed at the coincidence that one of the Welcome Wagon representatives would live right next door to him. And Mrs Hulka thought it must be just beautiful for Lauri to have a view of the swimming pool. It seemed like everybody was trying to dig up all the compliments they could about each other. They talked about the beautiful vistas from each of their terraces, the innumerable ecstasies of living in Fort Lee. Bobby was grateful he didn't have to say too much. Mrs Hulka had focused right on Lauri; and it didn't seem to matter what response he himself made to Mr Hulka's drunken slurs, because the slightest nod seemed to send Mr Hulka off into rather athletic physical motions and wide vocal ranges of amusement. In fact, Bobby came to the conclusion that he could just unabashedly examine the entire living-room with his eyes and Mr Hulka wouldn't notice any lack of audience. First, Bobby decided to check the three dolls' houses which were set up all along the far wall. He wanted to see them in more detail, particularly how intricately each one was fashioned, and in each house they had stiff little people dolls, each about four inches high. Each house had a little mother and a little father and a little son and a little daughter and a little dog. It was the worst taste Bobby had ever seen in dolls' houses. The only thing competing with the dolls' houses in the living-room decor was a long table boasting about twenty beautiful small boxes, each about a foot long, six inches high and eight inches wide. These were all made of polished dark inlaid wood. Everything else seemed to disappear in importance. The luxurious white sofa, the tan leather chairs, and the wall-to-wall green carpet; even the purple throw rug by the front door was lost from peripheral view when compared to all those small little boxes and the dolls' houses. Bobby forced himself to look at a few other details; there was some silver wallpaper in the hall that went down to where he knew the bedrooms were. In fact Bobby remembered climbing over the terrace and strolling around in the apartment when it had been empty for all those months until he knew where everything was, even the guest bathroom. There were a few Chinese urns and Dresden figurines now, and the huge RCA television console was rammed up against the south wall. But still everything seemed to disappear except the dolls' houses and the sparkling wooden boxes all in a row. That one wall lined with all those objects was the only thing that made the Hulka apartment different from any other nouveau riche gaudy living-room layout Bobby and Lauri had ever seen at the Century Tower.

'Oh! Oh! Look at the dolls' houses!' Bobby decided to feign surprise. He rushed over to them. 'Lauri, aren't they something!'

Lauri gave Bobby a disapproving look and made it quite clear that she thought that he should just shut up. If the Hulkas wanted to talk about their dolls' houses let *them* initiate the subject. As far as she was concerned, it was all very grotesque.

Bobby made even a bigger fuss. 'And look at all the little people living in them. Isn't it wonderful, Lauri?'

'Yes. Very wonderful.'

'Little mommies, and daddies, and sons, and daughters, and little baby animals,' Bobby fawned, taking the welcome sign from around his neck and placing it on the table next to one of the dolls' houses. 'Doesn't the sign look terrific here?'

Lauri got up from the sofa when she realized that the Hulkas were waiting for some kind of response from her. She moved slowly towards one of the dolls' houses that had a little boy near a tiny kitchen stove. 'Very unique,' she said, and she couldn't help thinking how each of them looked like homes that had been in an earthquake, where one wall just falls out. For a moment she had the strangest sensation that she was being drawn into the little world of one of the houses. Lauri-through-the-looking-glass, she thought to herself.

'They are very special to us,' Mrs Hulka remarked. 'So far we've got only the mansion, the Cape Cod, and the ranch, but we are hoping to add an A-frame.'

Just the word 'ranch' was enough to remind Lauri of the night the Kaminsky family died, and she felt a chill dance up the vertebrae of her spine. Bobby noticed her turn white and took her hand, turning her away from the dolls' houses. 'Boy, that sure is a beautiful view of the bridge, isn't it?' Bobby said, trying to change the subject. But Mr Hulka wasn't quite ready to let go.

'It's our hobby,' Mr Hulka said. 'We love carving, do all the miniature furniture by hand. There's a Victorian sofa in the Cape Cod that took Veronica a month to chisel and stitch.'

'What's in all the wooden boxes?' Bobby blurted, keeping Lauri turned away from the dolls' houses.

'I had nothing to do with those,' Veronica said, moving to a portable bar and pouring herself a fresh martini from a pitcher.

'Oh, they're my personal hobby,' Mr Hulka explained.

'I won't even touch them,' Mrs Hulka said, giving an exaggerated shiver and plopping into a hammock that was stretched across the corner of their living-room closest to the east terrace. '*I think they're really disgusting.*' She began to swing in a rather wide arc, stretched out, balancing her martini glass in the air. It was the first time Bobby had ever seen a hammock in a living-room and this one was colour co-ordinated with the drapes. When you're rich you can do just anything you want, Bobby thought, and they call it *flair*.

'That's a beautiful hammock,' Lauri said, her voice a little shaky.

Mrs Hulka twisted her head to look at Lauri. 'I like it because some days I just drag it right out on the terrace and swing to my heart's content. *I*,' she said, stressing the

I, 'love anything that's in motion. I love to be very much alive,' she added with innuendo, looking at her husband and still reflecting the fact that she really didn't like the little wooden boxes all lined up.

'What are the boxes?' Bobby pursued, noticing that Lauri's face was regaining colour.

'Vulgar, crass horrors,' Mrs Hulka shot out, giving herself an extra big swing and waving her legs to keep up the motion.

'*Veronica*,' Mr Hulka said with admonition, 'stop making a big thing about it. They are antique dissection kits. They are all from the 1800s, from most of the famous medical schools in Europe; from Padua, Bologna, and they are very valuable, made entirely of the most expensive woods, all blended and designed to contain some very beautiful silver instruments.'

'They have scalpels, bone crushers and skull saws.' Mrs Hulka burped loudly, an act which created a definite silence in the room. For a moment it was clear to both Bobby and Lauri that Mr Hulka's eyes were no longer looking as jolly as they had been. They were beginning to look *very* deep set – *and* very annoyed at his wife. Bobby decided that the best thing was to break the mood, so he pranced Lauri back to their seats on the sofa and launched straight into, 'What kind of work do you do, Mr Hulka?'

Mr Hulka broke his angry stare at Mrs Hulka. It even seemed he became aware that he had begun to grind his teeth. He suddenly relaxed and fell back into his laughing mood and sat in a charcoal-coloured suede chair near the console.

'What kind of work do you *think* I do?' he counter-questioned.

'Bobby, it's none of our business,' Lauri said.

'No, it's all right,' Mr Hulka assured.

'I think you're with a government agency,' Bobby announced.

'That's hilarious,' Mrs Hulka interjected, swinging out

46

of the hammock and starting to pace along the windows of the living-room. She was wearing an expression on her faultlessly painted face of an irritated cherub who needed just one more drink and she'd strap on a pair of haute couture wings and fly off the terrace.

'Well, we've got to be going,' Lauri said, getting up and heading for the door. 'It was a lot of fun welcoming you to Century Tower and we hope you have a long, healthy life here. The pool hours are from ten a.m. to six p.m., Monday through Friday, and it stays open until nine p.m. on Saturdays and Sundays. Bye-bye.'

Mr Hulka ignored Lauri and narrowed in on Bobby with heightened fascination. 'What makes you think I'm with the government?'

'Because you've got weird hours,' Bobby stated. 'I see you driving in and out at all sorts of times in that station-wagon with the black windows.'

'You're very observant,' Mr Hulka complimented him, and then glanced at his watch.

'I like to think I am,' Bobby said.

'Well, so long now,' Lauri mumbled. 'And don't forget, there's a great candy machine on level A in case you get the munchies while you're watching television.' Lauri couldn't take her eyes off Mrs Hulka. She looked so elegant and rich, like a prize cheetah pacing in a zoo. Lauri also got the feeling that Mr and Mrs Hulka didn't exactly like each other, but maybe, she thought, she was picking up the wrong vibes. Maybe she was just projecting, always ready to think the worst about things and objects and life in general.

'Actually,' Mr Hulka told Bobby, 'I'm on television.'

Bobby and Lauri looked at each other. 'Television?' Bobby echoed. 'You're *on* television?'

Mr Hulka looked at his watch and suddenly ran for the console. He swung open the large left door to reveal the television screen and snapped on a switch. Then he grabbed up a remote-control tuner from on top of the set and walked back, electronically changing the channels.

'I'm on the news,' he explained. 'I should be on right about now.'

'Big deal,' Mrs Hulka said.

'Do you *do* the six o'clock news?' Bobby asked. 'That's it, isn't it? You tape the six o'clock news. That's why you could be on right now.'

Mr Hulka started to laugh, but he didn't explain. Instead he kept switching the channels and then suddenly stopped and began to adjust the volume.

This is very freaky, Lauri thought to herself. This man is beginning to look crazy again, and wouldn't it be just awful if this was all Mr Hulka really did, that he was demented and spent most of his time in front of a television set, turning the dials, looking for himself? There was something crazy about that room with the dolls' houses and all the little boxes, and Mrs Hulka slithering and slapping the hammock back and forth. And now Mr Hulka suddenly saying he was on television. She was sure somehow, somewhere, she and Bobby were really going to be punished for this Welcome Wagon. Finally, even Bobby looked puzzled and uncomfortable.

'Here I am,' Mr Hulka blurted, and everybody held their breath, backing away, jockeying to get a view of the screen. Mr Hulka turned the volume up loud. He had cut in on the middle of a news segment and it was difficult to tell what was happening. There were a lot of people and a lady newscaster's voice was describing some kind of an event. Lauri strained to see if she could see Mr Hulka on the screen, but there were too many people. It was a church, and a large crowd on the steps and a lot of people in black were crying, theatrically sobbing. Flashbulbs were going off all over. Lauri moved a step forward when she heard the word 'widow' and the camera zoomed in for a close-up of an old lady wailing, being helped down the steps. The shot widened and then they could see Mr Hulka was there. She would recognize that face anywhere by now, even in a crowd on a television set. Mr Hulka was on the programme, dressed in black, and wearing a

48

yarmulke. He was on one side of the widow, helping support her. And the newscaster's voice was now making it clear that the old lady had lost her husband in a gangland killing. He had been found in cement in the East River. Her husband had been murdered. The camera cut to a different angle and you could see the lady reporter's face, with all the action going on in the background. She was giving all the grisly details about the cement covering only half the body, two or three bullets found in the back of the head; that he had been dumped in such shallow water that when the tide ran out he was discovered standing erect like some statuesque proof of inhumanity. But still in the background was Mr Hulka helping the widow into the limousine. Mr Hulka, smiling for the camera, constantly turning, aware of where the TV eyes were glaring. Mr Hulka looked very experienced. Then the camera swung to a shot of the hearse and flower car as the bereaved drove off, and that was the end of that item. Then some man came on and began to talk about the weather.

Mr Hulka reached out and turned the set off. He swung the door closed, hiding the screen, so that the console now seemed like one gigantic electronic dissection kit. He turned to face Lauri and Bobby and toasted them with his martini still in his left hand.

'I'm an undertaker,' he said, laughing rather irreverently.

Chapter 7

For the next couple of weeks Bobby and Lauri kept their meetings restricted to Lauri's terrace and the McDonald's hamburger emporium, which was just about a block and a half up the street from the Century Tower. McDonald's was, without a doubt, the favourite summer meeting place for all the kids from Fort Lee High, especially in the evening after the drive-ins let out, or the roller rinks were closed. Some kids would make a whole evening of just sitting at one of the outdoor tables and watching the traffic go by. There was hardly ever an empty table at the outdoor section, unless you got there very early. There were usually wall-to-wall teenagers eating Big Macs, french fries, and chocolate shakes. A lot of the times when Bobby and Lauri went to McDonald's, Bobby tried very hard to socialize, for Lauri's sake. He'd even smile at kids and try not to tell them off and sometimes they'd even say Hi back. But that's about as far as he could penetrate the cliques. He thought it would be good if Lauri had a few more friends to talk to. He didn't mind the fact that no one wanted to talk to him. Bobby felt guilty that he wasn't more successful about having kids come over to the table or letting them join them. He tried very hard to be tactful, in fact sometimes he'd deliberately take a big bite of a Quarter Pounder just to keep his mouth shut, hoping he'd be less offensive if he just chewed instead of talked. Another undercurrent that was lingering on was the fact that he felt a lot of guilt that he had put together a Welcome Wagon and called upon an undertaker with Lauri. He had no idea that an undertaker moved in right next door to him. He felt undertakers weren't even allowed to live in high-rise apartments. He thought they just lived in their funeral parlours or maybe slept in their casket showrooms, or things like that. He never knew anybody that had an undertaker living right next door to them. But the damage had already been done, so he tried to keep their conversation on anything except Jack and Veronica Hulka in 24G. He kept bringing up topics like the awful summer TV shows, the air quality ratings for the day, and a couple of times they made return trips to The Cloisters to see the fantastic Unicorn tapestries. They did other things, too. They took a few hikes down around the bottom of the cliffs and walked out on some of the piers. Once they even went down to the yacht club to look at some of the boats tied up there. Sometimes they would even see people water-skiing out on the Hudson River and Bobby thought seriously about hiring a boat. Still another time, the Perkinses let Bobby take Lauri with them for a visit to the Catskill Game Farm, and Bobby drove all the way, commanding the station-wagon with expertise. They even found a great pizza place in Kingston on that trip.

Sometimes, however, the topic of the Hulkas was unavoidable, like when they would be sitting on Lauri's terrace and Mr and Mrs Hulka would come out to mix at the pool. The Hulkas seemed to have about as much social success at the Century Tower pool as Lauri and Bobby had at McDonald's. Most of the tenants already knew Mr Hulka was an undertaker, because a few of the doormen had found out and the news had spread like wildfire.

Sunday, Wednesday and Friday afternoons, the Hulkas would usually appear at the pool around two o'clock. Lauri and Bobby were always in position, sipping their drink of the day, watching from the terrace above. No matter how crowded the pool was, Mr and Mrs Hulka never had any trouble finding a space.

'It's so sad,' Lauri said.

'What?' Bobby asked.

'Nobody really likes an undertaker,' Lauri clarified. 'Do you notice how nobody wants to sit next to them?' She was surprised to hear herself say such a thing.

But it really was pathetic to watch the way the Hulkas were treated. Granted, they showed up looking too flashy and Mr Hulka always wore a tight pair of red swimming trunks to show off his muscular body, and Mrs Hulka always wore a one-piece bathing suit that plunged much farther down her back than it had any right to. Her stiff blonde hair also looked quite out of place next to the pool and her sandals had colourful seashell clusters. Sometimes she fussed with a rainbow-coloured robe as though it were an ermine stole, and then she'd let it fall dramatically to reveal her cleavage. The first few times the Hulkas had appeared there were couples and families who didn't know anything about them and they were very friendly to begin with. Without even hearing the conversations going on below, Bobby and Lauri could tell the exact moment when the chitchat got around to occupations and Mr Hulka had to announce that he was an undertaker. Whosoever they were talking with would stiffen, begin to look nervous, and look for the first excuse to clear out and head for the other side of the pool. Sometimes they would even dive straight in the water to get away, as though to cleanse themselves. An advantage, however, of course, was that there was always a lot of room around the Hulkas for them to stretch out in the sun. It was clear Mrs Hulka would never go in the water. She was dressed just too expensively and her hair had too much money invested in it to go near anything like moisture. But Mr Hulka would run about and sometimes swim length after length of the pool, acting as though he was very, very youthful. The trouble was he seemed obsessed with acting youthful, almost desperate to appear young. It didn't seem right. His muscles were beginning to sag a little, but he still was in pretty good shape. The only thing that didn't look in good shape was his disposition and you could see he and Mrs Hulka were used to having a lot of arguments under their breath. She'd sometimes just turn him off entirely by flipping over on her stomach to avoid any further conversation with him.

'He looks like he's afraid of growing old,' Bobby commented one afternoon. 'I see a lot of guys around here, doing exercises, and they all have this terrified look on their faces, as though if they don't get rid of the tyre tube around their waist they're going to drop dead.'

'How do you know?' Lauri asked.

'I just know.'

Lauri sighed and took a sip of her drink right after they had noticed a particularly obvious rejection of the Hulkas. 'Why do you think people run away from them so quickly?'

'Well, the way I've got it figured,' Bobby said, 'is that they shake hands with *him* before they know he's an undertaker and then when he tells them what he does, they are all afraid that he's still covered with embalming fluid or old blood.'

'That's horrible,' Lauri said. 'I'm sure they have special cleaning fluids and rubber gloves so his hands stay clean.'

The rest of July Bobby and Lauri hardly even spoke about the Hulkas. They decided every time that topic came up it got just too morbid, so they just crossed them off their list. Even the first few days of August gave no promise that the summer was going to be anything more than one of the more tiresome ones Bobby and Lauri had each ever known. Bobby's folks had invited him and Lauri to go with them on a trip to Vermont, specifically to an obscure town called Middletown Springs where they were supposed to climb Mt Kilgore's ridges and store up on maple sugar – so they could have nice juicy waffles all winter. Bobby decided he didn't have enough energy for a whole two-week trip, so he just helped them pack the station-wagon and said goodbye and told them not to worry about anything.

'Just don't fall off any cliffs, and watch out for any noisy bears or rabid bats,' he advised. And so it was no big special event. Everything went on as usual with them gone. In fact, the first evening Bobby was going to be alone in the apartment, he took Lauri out to McDonald's and they got two Quarter Pounders with cheese, and managed to get one of the outside tables before all the other kids had taken over. One girl said hello to Lauri, but then she kept walking on her way. And then another boy came over and greeted Bobby, but Bobby could tell the kid was sort of putting him on and making up a really dumb story about he was going to take off to Paris to go quail hunting.

'You're a load of baloney,' Bobby said.

'And so are you,' the kid said. 'You jerk.'

Bobby would have got up and socked him right there and then, but the kid moved quickly and got into a car with some other kids and they all just let out donkey laughs as they drove off.

'Why do kids always make fun of me?' Bobby said.

'Because you tell them they're filled with baloney.'

'Well, they are.'

'So what do you care if they laugh at you then?'

'You're right, I don't care,' Bobby said. But Lauri knew he did.

The next morning Bobby slept until almost eleven and was faintly aware of noises coming from behind the walls – or through one of the air vents. While Bobby was in the kitchen opening a Yoo-hoo chocolate drink, he realized that there was a distinct argument going on somewhere. It was muffled so he didn't pay any real attention to it at first. It seemed to be a man and a woman talking quite loudly. For all he knew it could have been coming from a television set. Actually, it had to be coming from the Hulkas' apartment because there was nobody else on the floor. And that didn't surprise him anyway. He figured they had lots of fights. Probably the only reason he didn't hear more of them was because the walls were thick – an unusual feature in most modern high rises. He had just pressed an English muffin into the toaster when suddenly the woman's voice began to rise in volume, and although he still couldn't make out the exact words, he knew it was the loudest voice he had ever heard at the Century Tower. Then he could make out Mr Hulka's voice booming and he was ready to put on the radio to drown out the whole thing, but there was something about it that made him feel there was more than a family squabble going on. It wasn't any little argument about how to carve a new dolls' house, or wax an old dissection kit. In fact, what was going on over there seemed to be going beyond words. They seemed to be going into the area of shrieks and suddenly a cry, a scream cut short. Bobby was still sort of waking up so he thought maybe it was just part of his imagination, but then there was a real thud against the kitchen wall. For some reason the hair bristled on the back of his neck, and he started to whistle and took the English muffin out and buttered it. But then there was another sound, glass breaking. Just an accident, he told himself. A vase had fallen, and that was it. A vase in the Hulkas' apartment, one of those probably on the long table when you came in, or maybe it was a piece of Steuben glass on the television set. Nevertheless, Bobby went to yank open the door to his terrace but the lock was on. He needed to move the tiny lever up and then he swung the Thermopane door open. He found himself tiptoeing to the partition, and then, before he could help himself, he was peeking around and into the Hulkas' living-room. He could see the hammock in the one corner, silent and still. He moved his head farther out and could catch a glimpse of the sofa and elephant end tables – and then there, at the very far end of the living-room, was Mr Hulka, his face distorted, his arms thrust downward on to something. It looked as though he was pressing on a sack of some sort. It was white fur, a lot of very white fur, and Bobby stretched his neck farther and farther until he could see on top of this massive white fur the stiff blonde hair that he had seen so often on Mrs Hulka. Mr Hulka was straining as though he was trying to break a drumstick off a turkey, and his hands looked like they were grasping, choking something. In a moment, the whole mass was in motion. The white fur, the hair, it was all in Mr Hulka's arms, looking like a limp animal. And then there was a pair of legs protruding, with high heels, and Mr Hulka carried his burden down the hall which Bobby knew led to the master bedroom. Then no matter how far Bobby leaned forward, he could see nothing farther along the far wall than the lifeless inner sanctums of the dolls' houses.

Instinctively, even surprising himself, Bobby grabbed one of the Perkinses' aluminium terrace chairs from behind him and threw it around the partition. It landed with a loud clatter, scraping along the cement of the Hulkas' terrace, bouncing off the impenetrable Thermopane glass doors. Bobby knew there was no way Hulka couldn't have heard the noise, and if he hadn't already done something brutally irreversible to his wife, he thought the sound might bring him to his senses. He would have to know that he was seen. He would have to know that someone from over on the Perkinses' terrace had heard what was going on and had done something about it, that someone *would* do something about it. Bobby ran at breakneck speed to the telephone. A million thoughts shot through his head. Maybe Hulka had just rendered her unconscious, slapped her around and choked her. Maybe that was even the standard way they had their fights. Maybe he was taking her into the bedroom just to bring her around. Maybe it wasn't what he thought it was, what it looked like. He realized he had slammed his terrace door behind him and automatically put on the lock, and he felt his blood rushing up to his head, almost deafening him as he reached the kitchen and grabbed for the phone. He kept an eye on the terrace as he dialled. BOBBY PERKINS FOILS MURDER WITH CHAIR. And he even revised that to read, BOY HOLDS BEAST AT BAY WITH LAWN CHAIR.

'Hello?' came Lauri's voice on the phone.

Bobby hesitated speaking. Already he was sorry he had even dialled the number. He didn't want to mix her up in this but it was too late.

'Hello? Hello?' Lauri's voice repeated.

Bobby spoke. 'I think he just knocked her off,' he blurted.

'What?' Lauri asked. 'Bobby, is that you?'

'Yes,' Bobby said. 'I think Hulka just knocked off his wife.'

'Bobby, it's too early for a joke. Come on down and have some Special K.'

'Lauri, I'm serious! Call the cops!'

'Bobby, I don't think this is very funny.'

'Look, he might jump around the terrace any minute and come after me. I threw a chair over there.'

'You threw a chair?'

'Lauri, have your mother call.'

'Bobby, are you practising a scene?'

Bobby practically gagged, so many words began to collect in his throat. 'Lauri, you're the last one I want to have to think about this, but get somebody to call the cops. They won't believe me. Get the doorman, the super, anybody. Get them up here. I can't talk any more. Just tell them and then make believe I didn't call and go back to sleep.'

'Are you *sure*?' Lauri asked.

'Just call,' Bobby ordered. 'I've got to get over there and check it out.'

'Don't!' Lauri screamed into the receiver as Bobby hung up.

But Bobby was already having a frantic conversation with himself. 'I have to go find out. It's my duty.' He started to bump into furniture, not knowing whether he should try swinging out around the partition, pretend he was Tarzan or Bomba the jungle boy, and start banging on the windows. He knew he needed a sledgehammer to break them, or even a regular hammer if he swung real hard. He saw his mother's small butane torch and thought about picking that up and running over there, but he figured that would take about eight hours to cut through anything in case the terrace doors were locked. Then, before he knew how, he found himself at the door to the hallway and for a moment he was going to swing it wide open, but he realized Hulka could be waiting right out there in the hall. He could have heard the chair crash out on the terrace, *knowing that it was Bobby home alone*. He could have known that the Perkinses had gone off camping. His eyes shot up and he saw the long screwdriver with the plastic yellow handle and he grabbed that and held it like a knife. Then he threw the door open anyway and even if Hulka's hands were to come shooting into view, he'd take the screwdriver and start jabbing, only in self-defence, of course. For a moment the headline came – BOBBY PERKINS SCREWDRIVERS MALICIOUS UNDERTAKER TO DEATH. But the hallway was empty. Silent as usual. There was no reason to go banging on all the other doors because there was nobody behind them, and there was no time to run up and down all the flights, using the exit stairs at the far end. There wasn't time to wait for the elevator. There wasn't time to do anything, not even throw a water balloon off the terrace with a note attached to it. There was nothing to do except act as though he was in school and be as pushy as he usually was, so he went right to the Hulkas' door and grabbed the doorknob. Part of him hoped it would refuse to turn, that there would be nothing but a hundred locks stopping the thing from revolving. He knew the better part of valour would be to wait for the elevator doors to open and Lauri would have a salvation posse galloping to help him. But the knob did turn and the door did open. Fortunately, it was Bobby's energy that committed the act and not Mr Hulka on the other side of the door, getting ready to work him over with the contents of a dissection kit or sock him on the head with a dolls' house or shoot his hands under Bobby's throat like he had done to Mrs Hulka. 'Please don't be killing her,' he found himself saying under his breath. 'Please don't be killing her,' as he pushed the door all the way open.

Bobby paused at the entranceway. Quickly he swung a chair to keep the door open just in case he had to make like a roadrunner and get out of there in a hurry. Maybe he had been seeing things. Maybe somewhere his sleep got mixed up with the English muffin and the Yoo-hoo and the events were all out of sequence. He started to trespass farther inside but stopped in the middle of the ugly purple rug of the hallway. Its colour seemed to scream at him louder than ever. There was only one change in the apartment since he had been peering around the partition. The door to the master bedroom had been closed. He didn't have to actually see, he told himself. He didn't need to look down that hallway towards the bedroom, and the huge bathroom and the walk-in closet he knew were there. He didn't have to go any closer to know Mr Hulka would be waiting to leap at him. He again held the screwdriver out in front of him, getting ready to thrust it out like a horizontal pneumatic drill. All he knew was he had to help Mrs Hulka if it wasn't too late, and suddenly he found himself yelling, 'Don't kill her, Hulka! Don't kill her! I saw you, and the cops are coming! They're coming! I called everybody and they're going to come and get you! Don't kill her!'

Then he realized the horrific possibility that maybe Lauri thought it was just one more game and she was on her way up by herself. Bobby could get knocked off and then Lauri would just come walking in and she would get knocked off and then there would be a bunch of corpses in there and God only knows what Hulka would do with them. If there was anybody who would certainly know how to get rid of a corpse and not get caught it would be an undertaker. Bobby began to back out towards the hall door, back over the purple throw rug, but then it also occurred to him that maybe Mr Hulka had already swung out from his terrace, around the partition and had gone into the Perkinses' apartment and now he could be ready to jump out of the Perkinses' apartment and ambush him. When it came right down to it, Bobby didn't know where Hulka was. He could be in front of him or behind him. But then he remembered he had locked his own terrace door, so there was no way Hulka could get through that without making a crash so loud it would sound like an explosion. But there were other partitions and other terrace doors and maybe Hulka was out there swinging like a baboon from terrace to terrace until he found a door that was open, and now he might pop out of any of the doors.

Suddenly there was a swooshing sound at Bobby's back as though a large bird was flapping its wings and hurtling forward in attack.

Chapter 8

Bobby turned to see that the elevator doors at the far end of the corridor had opened. People were running towards him. Lauri was leading the crowd. Behind her were two policemen, and bringing up the rear was a mean doorman he and Lauri had nicknamed 'Joe the Schmo'. He was always so negative and he looked just like a nasty little dwarf in a baggy blue uniform, something left over from a Marx Brothers film who deserved to get a good pie in the face.

'Are you okay?' Lauri called as she was still rushing forward. In a second she was at Bobby's side.

'Yes, thanks,' he said with relief. Then he was flanked by the policemen who took on more precise definition: the tall, coldly efficient Patrolman Petrie whom Bobby knew very well from past adventures, and Petrie's buddy who looked exactly like Sergeant Collins's younger brother. The emotion both policemen showed was primarily boredom.

'What's the problem?' Officer Petrie sighed.

Bobby pointed towards the bedroom door. 'There's a mortician in there. Hulka. Mr Hulka. He did something to his wife. He started choking her and he carried her off in this big white fur and she's got stiff blonde hair and he's done something to her inside there.' Bobby was aware that his grammar was not entirely perfect at this moment, but he felt he had conveyed some sense of the urgency of the moment, although the policemen still looked deeply unimpressed. He began to realize he would have to get a little more sensational about it and use some superlatives to get the men in blue to react at all. 'I saw his hands digging right into her throat and he was shoving her and pounding on her and then he was dragging her like

Mr Hyde and he was foaming from the mouth.' He reached out and grabbed Lauri's hand because he realized that she was beginning to look very frightened. He didn't know whether she was frightened because she believed everything he was saying or because she thought maybe he had lost his sanity and was bringing storytelling to a new high. Both policemen continued to breathe normally, looking quite ready to go' to sleep. The one that looked like Sergeant Collins's brother was the only one who really reacted. His head turned a quarter of an inch to look at the dolls' houses and the little boxes lined up against the wall, as though he was shopping for toys.

'Who let you in here?' Officer Petrie asked in a monotone as he took a pad out of his pocket.

'I let myself in. I turned the knob and the door was open,' Bobby said. He slipped the screwdriver into his back pocket where only its handle protruded. 'What does it matter how I got in here? Just stop the guy. Get into that bedroom.'

Joe the Schmo began to adjust his huge uniform jacket and he was talking a mile a minute, saying Bobby Perkins had always been a troublemaker at the Century Tower, that he did things like throw water missiles off the roof, and pressed multiple buttons on the elevators to inconvenience other passengers. Joe the Schmo added that Mr and Mrs Hulka, who lived in this apartment, were very respectable people and that Bobby was the kind of kid who deserved a couple of years in a reformatory. Bobby couldn't believe his ears. In one minute Joe the Schmo was blurting more black exposition about Bobby than Bobby himself could even remember. He was getting accused of everything in the neighbourhood. And Joe the Schmo did the thing he was famous for. He let a little spit fly out of the corner of his mouth. In addition to Joe the Schmo's other faults he was also a drooler and he would have gone on defaming Bobby and Lauri if the bedroom door hadn't opened at just that point. Mr Hulka stood before them, his eyes filling with surprise.

'I thought I heard voices out here,' Mr Hulka said calmly, entering and moving towards the group. He gently brushed the corners of a handkerchief he now wore in a jacket pocket and looked as though he was about to do a very chic men's cologne advertisement. 'Is there a fire?' he enquired innocently.

Officer Petrie's voice remained spiritless, reciting Bobby's charges. 'The boy here says you killed your wife. He says he saw you choke her and then drag her in there.' He pointed towards the bedroom hall.

Mr Hulka looked at Bobby. Bobby watched very closely for every reaction. Mr Hulka seemed to be playing the quality of surprise but Bobby got a whole new image of the man. It wasn't just Mr Hulka's eyes that seemed sinister. There was something else. His nose was slightly bent and his left nostril just a speck larger than his right. His hair now seemed darker than he had ever noticed before. Short, but not too short, almost Roman in the way a few black curls crept around over towards his heavy eyebrows, each of which seemed composed of two slashes of night meeting in a peak. His lips were also slightly offset, looking as though they were a pair of scissors. and his neck was a column of muscle with a windpipe that would take an axe to penetrate it. Bobby was also aware that the man no doubt looked normal upon first inspection by the police officers. It took quite a while of observation before anyone could see that this was the kind of face you would usually see in a newspaper about some maniac being caught in Michigan for hacking eleven co-eds to death. And what was worse was his performance of great amazement when Mr Hulka turned his full gaze back to the police.

'That's very interesting,' Mr Hulka said, beckoning for the police to come in farther into the living-room area. 'I'm afraid the boy has a bit of an imagination – and the girl, for that matter.'

'Leave her out of this,' Bobby said.

'I'm very sorry, Mr Hulka,' Joe the Schmo piped up,

starting to wipe his chin at last. 'She came screaming down the lobby and the police were giving tickets to those cars that block the garage. I warned everybody.'

'That's okay, Joe,' Mr Hulka insisted. 'It's very funny.'

'Well, I have to get back down on the door,' Joe the Schmo explained to the police. 'Is that okay with you guys?'

Patrolman Petrie nodded affirmatively. 'But,' Joe continued, 'I want to tell you, both of these kids are right off the wall! They are Looney Tunes! They always have been!' He began to point like a metronome at Bobby and Lauri.

'You're the one off the wall,' Bobby told him.

Old Joe just gave Bobby a look like he wanted to take out a cheap bottle of wine and hit him over the head. Instead he just *harrumphed* and marched out, closing the door behind him.

Bobby decided not to let any of the momentum stop. 'Mr Hulka had his hands around Mrs Hulka's throat and he was pressing so hard and his face became twisted and she was wearing a white fur coat and she's got fancy blonde hair and he choked her and choked her and choked her and then dragged her into that room – *you just go right in there, right this minute, her body's right in there!* Mrs Hulka! Mrs Hulka!' Bobby began to call out.

Officer Petrie stopped jotting in his pad and looked coldly at Bobby. 'And how did you manage to see all of this activity?' he enquired.

'From my terrace,' Bobby said. pointing out towards Mr Hulka's terrace and then swinging his hand around. 'I live right next door and I'll tell you, I'm really thankful that at last someone's here, but you've got to get in that room right now. Maybe you can give her mouth-to-mouth resuscitation. Hurry up. Somebody's got to help her.' He felt Lauri press closer to him and that gave him even more support.

'This boy and girl have very fanciful projects,' Mr Hulka launched into. 'They both arrived here a few weeks ago pretending to be representatives of a "Welcome Wagon" and my wife and I were very polite to them. Were we not?' Mr Hulka elicited, turning to Bobby and Lauri, his left nostril expanding.

Bobby paid no attention. 'I heard a thud from my apartment and a crash of glass.' Bobby spun to look against the Hulkas' wall. 'Yeah, look, *there*. See. Broken glass.'

'Yes, I dropped a jardinière,' Mr Hulka said calmly. 'That did fall this morning by accident, and that was the sound you heard, young man.'

'I don't think so,' Bobby corrected. 'What you don't know is I can look right around and see most of your living-room from my terrace, and I saw him going at her like he was wringing a chicken's neck!' Suddenly Bobby was so exasperated he couldn't stop himself. 'One of you police jerks just go in there! She's dead! Look for her! Get her! She's in white and all this sticky blonde hair!'

'He didn't mean to call you jerks,' Lauri apologized to the policemen.

'They *are* jerks,' Bobby reiterated.

'You'd better watch your mouth,' Officer Petrie said. Then he looked at Mr Hulka who was now laughing quite openly and waving his permission. 'Search anywhere you like, but something's got to be done about these kids. I mean, this is harmless now, but they must be quite a nuisance to other people in the building.' Officer Petrie walked quickly down the hall to the bedroom.

'Watch him,' Bobby warned the Officer Collins lookalike, making it quite clear he meant Hulka. 'I'd draw my gun if I were you and hold it at his head.'

Mr Hulka looked at Bobby and now his eyes really meant business. 'Why, you're rather sadistic, aren't you, young man?'

Bobby glared right back at him. '*You're* the killer!'

'You just shut your mouth, kid,' the officer said.

All eyes then turned to the bedroom doorway and there was Officer Petrie, expressionless and ready with his report. He silently reached his hand out towards Bobby and beckoned him with one finger to come forward. Bobby moved towards him with Lauri still holding his hand, tiptoeing behind him.

'You'd better stay here,' Bobby told her.

Lauri only clung tighter to him.

In a moment they were all in position next to Officer Petrie, staring down the hall to the master bedroom. There at the far end was the form of a woman standing, supporting a long white coat. A stiff blonde wig hovered just above. Lauri and Bobby both stiffened for a moment when they saw that the woman had no eyes, no nose, no mouth. Her countenance was a faceless, appalling oval. It was a dressing dummy wearing only the white fur and the blonde wig and even Lauri had to let out a laugh of relief. Lauri let go of Bobby's hand and clapped with joy and even Officer Petrie had to start chuckling. Mr Hulka roared and curiosity finally got the best of the Officer Collins look-alike who moved into position to get a look. Soon everyone was laughing except Bobby. The big joke was over and Lauri took Bobby's hand again just to let him know he shouldn't feel embarrassed. He did what he thought he should have done.

Bobby looked at the policeman, and then at Mr Hulka. 'I saw you choking your wife,' Bobby said. 'Not that dummy. I saw a body in your arms, a body that bent when it was dragged. Your wife's body is still in there.' He addressed the cops with an urgency. 'He's got it under the bed or in the shower or tied up behind the drapes or in a closet, or maybe she's swinging over the edge or he threw her off the bedroom terrace. I don't know, but find her! *Hurry up and find her!*' He began to tremble. 'Maybe she isn't dead yet. Maybe he only choked her unconscious.' Bobby was now practically incoherent. 'That dummy's a dummy,' Bobby accused. Bobby looked at everyone, who all looked surprised at his latest outcry. Even Lauri couldn't conceal her puzzlement. Bobby let go of her hand and pushed Officer Petrie out of the way. He rushed into the bedroom, opening closets, looking in

66

bathrooms and shoving curtains aside.

'Get him.' Officer Petrie signalled the Officer Collins look-alike.

Bobby was soon aware of being restrained, of being halted in his movements. He just kept saying, 'He killed her. I know he killed her.' And his eyes kept darting this way and that. In a flash, Lauri was at his side again, trying to calm him down, saying, 'Look, forget it. You made a mistake. It's okay. You see, it's a dummy and there's that white coat. It's just a white rabbit coat. It's not a body. It's an easy mistake to make. Don't feel badly about it. It's okay.' The cops were yelling all sorts of things and then somewhere in the back of all of this confusion Bobby became aware of a woman's voice. It wasn't Lauri's voice. It was a mature lady's voice, faintly familiar, a little arched. He was being led back up the bedroom hall-way and into the living-room where he could hear Mr Hulka starting his explanation, convincingly, his deep voice soothingly explaining that he was an undertaker and that the kids had been so cute, bringing veal parmigiana and a cassata cake, but obviously his occupation had upset them and worked on their minds *and the Perkins boy had problems*; and the lady's voice was saying things like, 'Well, it *is* amusing. It certainly *is* amusing.' By the time Bobby had been propelled into the living-room he saw that the woman's voice belonged to Mrs Hulka. Mrs Hulka was standing there. She was very much alive. She was very upright. And she was very well. She was in no way dead. Bobby blinked his eyes. He was speechless for a change. It wasn't a robot! It was a living, breathing Mrs Hulka – and not even a chance it was a twin unless it had been cloned directly from a Mrs Hulka egg!

As usual, Mrs Hulka was impeccably dressed, taking off her small tasteful hat in front of the foyer mirror. 'I was picking up the accounting books from the parlour,' Mrs Hulka said. 'The *disgusting* parlour, and I don't want anybody to think that I *like* being the wife of an under-taker. I'd be prouder if he was in garbage. Jack can't add a jot, so I have to do all the inventory, and I had bought some cream-filled doughnuts, but really, *really* –' and this time she turned and directed it right at Lauri and Bobby – 'I'm not dead, children. I'm not dead at all. But thank you for caring.'

Officer Petrie gave a wink to the Hulkas and escorted Bobby and Lauri out into the hall. He closed the door and then verbally assailed Bobby. 'If they wanted to press charges against you for trespassing, you'd end up in juvenile court so fast you wouldn't know what hit you. Where are your parents?'

'They're not home,' Bobby said. 'They're on vacation.'

'Do they know they left behind a son who can't be trusted?'

'No, they don't, because I *can* be trusted.'

'He's not a troublemaker,' Lauri protested. 'You can ask my mother and father.'

'Where do you live?' Petrie threw at her.

'Three-A.'

'Leave her out of this, I told you,' Bobby insisted.

Lauri felt her brow getting moist and this time Bobby held *her* hand until she was finally able to speak. 'My mother is shopping at Cheese Heaven and my father works until five at the Hoboken Smelting Works.'

Officer Petrie sucked in a great breath of air, swelling his rib cage to almost twice its size. 'You think I don't remember you two? Do you think cops are stupid? I remember you with the monkey masks on the bridge – and if you aren't roasting marshmallows you're always shoving wienies on a fire – and you know you're not supposed to build fires out on the cliffs. And maybe you think it's funny getting dressed up like monks and nuns, but I don't, because I happen to be a Catholic.'

'We weren't making fun of anything,' Lauri said.

'We were portraying medieval religious figures,' Bobby specified. 'We weren't making fun of any religion. Besides, we were on stage. We were practising in case we ever really decided to become very religious, and there's nothing wrong with practising.'

'The whole stationhouse knows you two crazies,' Petrie continued to blast. 'Your folks are just like all the other brats' parents today. They don't even care about you.'

'You're the crazy one,' Bobby said. 'Our folks love us!'

Officer Petrie ignored them and launched into, 'You kids think you can mug, kill and freak out, and us cops are the ones that have to get stuck doing what your mothers and fathers should have done to you – beat the hell out of you when you were little runts! Now the courts have to use taxpayers' money to make you snots understand that you're not going to run this world.'

'Ha!' Bobby blurted out, and Lauri started to bend his thumb as a signal for him to shut up. 'Ha!' Bobby repeated. 'My folks are the same taxpayers who fork over all the loot so you guys can go coop in your patrol cars, and take four-hour lunch breaks. We see you taking snoozes down by the river.'

'You think it's a big joke, getting us over here, don't you?' Officer Petrie said, lowering his voice and somehow becoming more threatening. 'A nice big joke to pull on an undertaker. And you're the big puncher, aren't you?' he said, suddenly remembering. 'The big puncher from the block party! Well, let me tell you something, I'll put out an all-states bulletin and yank your parents back here so quick they'll lock you in a closet for a year! And *you*,' he went on, almost touching Lauri's nose, 'your mother won't be able to buy a Kraft cheese spread, much less go shopping at Cheese Heaven. Your father will be on overtime to pay for the lawyers you're going to need. Why don't you ingrates go out and get a job? Why don't you work and find out what it's like to earn a living?'

'*Because there are no jobs*,' Bobby said factually. 'Or haven't you heard of unemployment?'

'Baloney,' Officer Petrie belched.

'And liverwurst to you!'

Lauri was lifting her hand almost ready to clap it over Bobby's mouth when Officer Collins's look-alike came out of the Hulkas' apartment carrying the aluminium terrace chair. He motioned it towards Bobby. 'You threw this?' Officer Petrie grabbed the chair and his face turned scarlet. 'We send kids like you to pea farms, you destructive little skunk!'

Bobby had his mouth wide open and was ready to yell bloody murder, but Lauri jerked his arm so much that his head practically bounced off his own shoulder. Lauri held on to him tightly as Petrie finished another barrage of threats. At last the lecture was over and Bobby and Lauri were allowed to go back into Bobby's apartment, leaving the officers standing in the hall.

'We *are* very sorry,' Lauri said, once Bobby was safely within the threshold.

'Yes, we *are* very sorry,' Bobby said, grabbing hold of the door with both hands and slamming it with such force he hoped the noise would sting the policemen's eardrums. The slam reverberated inside the Perkinses' apartment, but at last Lauri and Bobby were alone. They waited a minute to see if the police were going to ring the buzzer or try to break down the door, but they didn't. It looked like at last they were going to have a little peace and quiet, so Lauri moved into the kitchen and poured two club sodas. She got a lemon out of the refrigerator and sliced a couple of wedges. By the time she came back into the living-room Bobby was just sitting on the sofa with his feet up on the coffee table, sulking. He was fondling the big screwdriver with the yellow plastic handle, and Lauri thought he looked angry enough to throw it across the room. She took it away from him and put it back up on the stereo rigging near the front door. She also knew when Bobby needed a few minutes to be alone to calm down, so she just stood by the hall mirror and checked her face for any telltale signs of terror. Then by the time she rejoined him he was no longer cursing to himself. He just sat on the sofa, holding the cold glass on the side of his right temple. She waited another minute but realized he still wasn't ready to talk, so she went into the kitchen and found some pretzels and put them in a bowl. Then she came back almost singing. 'That's an easy mistake to make,' Lauri said. She set the pretzels down and began chewing. 'It's really a beautiful day out. The sun is terrific and the view is just gorgeous. There was a fog under the bridge at dawn but then it all moved out. Oh my!' she said, turning and looking out the window towards the bridge. 'Look how heavy the traffic is already.'

Finally, Bobby broke his silence. 'Did you notice anything unusual?'

'Like what?' Lauri asked.

'About over *there*,' Bobby said, pointing towards the wall. 'About the Hulkas' joint.'

Lauri thought very hard. She furrowed her brow and pinched her lips together and thought and thought. 'No.'

Bobby took a sip of his soda water and stared into the glass for a long time and then set it down. 'I saw him kill somebody.'

'But Mrs Hulka *is* alive. You saw her holding the account books and the box from Donut King.'

Bobby looked at her. 'Yeah. That means he killed somebody else.'

'Who?'

'How do *I* know?'

Lauri filled up with oxygen to launch what had to be said. 'Look, Bobby. It's no coincidence, that white rabbit fur stuck on that dummy and with the wig, you know. Mrs Hulka probably has twenty different wigs.'

'No, she doesn't. That's her real hair she wears.'

'Maybe she has wigs for sometimes, when we don't see her.'

'But that coat. I tell you there was a real woman in it because the arms were hanging and Hulka was carrying it and it was a body. And that body has got to still be over there! Didn't you notice anything deranged at all, *anything weird*?'

'No,' Lauri said. 'Besides, this is summertime, so nobody's going to wear a fur coat. So the natural place for a fur coat is going to be on a dummy.'

'Why?'

'Sometimes you've got to check them for moths, or do repairing on them. Especially rabbit furs. They're very cheap. I know, because I was going to buy one last Christmas. My mother said I could have a rabbit coat or my own clock-radio. I decided I wanted the clock-radio.'

'So you didn't notice anything weird.'

'Bobby,' Lauri said, 'once you've seen the dolls' houses and the antique dissection kits, nothing's going to look weird.' Then Lauri added, 'There *was* a smell. It was the smell of gardenias. And the other thing I noticed was that Mr Hulka looked like he wanted to hurt you. And maybe the smell wasn't gardenias. It could have been something they call tuberose. I read a short story once where a woman wore nothing but tuberose which is a fragrance that's supposed to mask the smell of corpses, and they use it in all the best funeral parlours. But I really think it smelled more like gardenias.' She noticed that Bobby was hanging on every word, so she decided that she had better go on. 'And then in the bedroom I saw Mrs Hulka's make-up on the vanity table. She had Chanel Number Five perfume, which doesn't smell like gardenias, and the already-mentioned rabbit fur coat, and all I was thinking was how horrible it was that Mrs Hulka had all those little rabbits killed. That was the real reason I got the clock-radio instead of the coat. I couldn't go walking around with all those little dead animals hanging all over me. She talks about the funeral parlour being disgusting but I think she's a walking *pet* funeral parlour. All those cute little bunnies that had to be slaughtered, and . . .'

Bobby suddenly bolted upright and motioned Lauri to stop talking. He kept his head cocked at an angle, listening. In a moment he thought he was mistaken, but then the voices became clearer. It was like a case of déjà vu. Voices again, coming from behind the wall and through the vents. Bobby grabbed Lauri by the hand and ran with her into the kitchen. The man's voice was muffled and clear but the woman's voice was shrill. This time it was definitely Mrs Hulka and as Bobby's eyes caught the sight of his cold English muffin abandoned on the plate, he really felt like he was in some strange TV rerun.

'They're at it again,' he said. 'They're doing combat again. That's like when he killed her this morning.'

'But he *didn't* kill her this morning,' Lauri said.

'You don't hear them?'

'Sure, I hear them. She's screaming something . . . about a coat?' Lauri said as a question within a statement. 'Isn't that what she's shrieking about?'

Bobby bounded to the terrace doors and checked to make sure that the lock was open before he yanked. Lauri was right behind him and they dashed to the partition. Their heads were on top of each other, like a totem pole of two. This time the Hulkas' drapes were closed. Bobby turned and ran back into the kitchen. Lauri was scurrying at his heels and they got there just in time to hear a genuine scream. This was a scream that Bobby had heard only in some of the very best fright flicks. It wiggled its way through the cement as though the entire wall and air-conditioning slits were set in vibration, and this time the hair on the back of Bobby's head shot straight out like porcupine bristles. Then there was silence. Dead silence.

'He's really done her in this time,' Bobby whispered.

Lauri shifted from foot to foot. It was definitely a terrible scream. 'Maybe they're playing a joke on us now,' she offered weakly, although she didn't believe it. She knew it wasn't the kind of sound any wife would emit when her husband mildly disapproves of her choice of doughnuts or ledger procedures. This time Lauri, too, for a moment had the distinct feeling that Mrs Hulka had been punished. She found herself shaking because she realized the last time she had heard a scream like that was when there had been, that evening, the fire, the silhouettes of the Kaminskys frantic on window shades before it was too late. 'Maybe this time we had better call the police,' Lauri said, feeling a bit faint and staggering out into the living-room. This time *she* plopped on to the sofa.

'But they just left,' Bobby reminded her, walking to the doorway and noticing Lauri's face had turned as white as a cauliflower. 'Look,' he said, 'Lauri, don't you even think about this. You just lie there and think of a tropical beach or going on a disco tour of London. Think of anything not grim,' he commanded.

'It's just an anxiety attack,' Lauri said quietly. 'Don't even pay it any attention. Just call the police.'

Bobby ran to the phone. 'Don't listen. Pretend I'm booking two tickets for us to go to Mardi Gras in Brazil, okay?' His hand was a little unsteady as he dialled. It turned out to be a male operator.

'Hello. I'd like to speak to the police,' Bobby said.

'You can dial that direct,' the operator informed him. 'Nine-One-One.'

'Look, somebody's been murdered!' Bobby bellowed tactlessly.

The operator cleared his throat. 'Don't you yell at me, buster.'

'Look, mister,' Bobby exclaimed, 'I've got Jack the Ripper next door, and you get me those cops right now, you hear me? *Jack the Ripper!*'

'Good,' the operator said, 'I hope he gets you.'

Bobby heard the operator disconnect on him. He was furious but he held in there and punched 911 like each depression was a sock on that operator's jaw.

'Police Department,' a gruff male voice answered.

'I want to report a murder.' Bobby got right to the point.

'*Who is this?*'

Lauri could feel the blood coming back into her face. She moved into a normal sitting position trying to give Bobby at least support in the form of body language.

Bobby suddenly covered the receiver and mouthed a sentence to Lauri. 'It's Officer Petrie.' Then he put the phone back to his ear.

'Who is this?' he heard Officer Petrie's voice repeat.

'Bobby Perkins,' Bobby admitted. 'Listen, Mr Hulka really did something to Mrs Hulka this time. I'm not kidding. I know you're not going to believe it and everything, but it really happened. This is Officer Petrie, right?'

'Yes,' the voice said. 'I just got back here at the stationhouse,' he added. 'And I have made the mistake of answering this Mickey Mouse phone.'

'Look, I know it sounds crazy,' Bobby said, 'and maybe I was wrong the last time, but this time I really mean it. You've got to get over here. You should have heard the scream. He was tying her throat off like the end of a balloon.' There was a long silence on the end of the phone. Lauri looked at Bobby and Bobby looked at Lauri. He just kept waiting for Officer Petrie to react.

'You think Mr Hulka has killed Mrs Hulka?' Officer Petrie's voice enquired with a strange inflection, adding, 'Again?'

'I think so,' Bobby confided.

'I heard the scream, too,' Lauri yelled out towards the receiver.

Again there was a long pause. The only sound Bobby could hear was as if Officer Petrie was having an asthma attack. This time when Officer Petrie's voice arrived through the receiver it almost shattered a bone in Bobby's ear. 'I am down here filling out a report on how our time was wasted this morning on you wise guys, and I can tell you if we come up there again it's only going to be to put the two of you in jail until your folks show up! You got that?'

'Oh, but you don't understand,' Bobby started. 'You see, *this* time . . .'

'In fact,' Officer Petrie's voice interrupted thunderingly, 'if you call us one more time, or you trick anyone else into calling us within the next five years, about anybody murdering anybody, you two are going to get stuck in a sanatorium for the teenage insane.'

There was a click and Bobby was left holding a dead line. He looked at the receiver and then hung up.

'They didn't believe you?' Lauri asked.

'You might say that,' Bobby admitted.

Lauri sighed. 'Well, maybe there is a limit to the number of times you can report a guy executing his wife on the same day.'

'Well, what can we do?' Bobby asked.

Lauri didn't have an answer for that one right off the bat so she just took a sip of her club soda. She even fetched out the lemon wedge and bit into it, hoping the sourness of it would convince her that she was in reality. Bobby grabbed his lemon wedge and joined her, eating rind and all, while erupting with all the possible paths of action, all the alternatives.

'What are we going to do? Peep over the Hulkas' terrace again, start banging on the windows, throw some more lawn chairs?' Bobby offered.

'I don't know,' Lauri said.

'Maybe he didn't lock his terrace door. Shall we just sling it open and go running in? Or split down the hall and jump in the elevator and start ringing bells until we can find somebody who's going to believe us? And I don't mean *Joe the Schmo*.'

'I don't know,' Lauri repeated.

Bobby went on and on – everything from how they could storm the Hulkas' apartment or call the Governor or somebody who cared, the PAL, the YMCA, B'nai B'rith, the Undertakers' Association of America, the *Casket Quarterly*. 'I mean, there must be somebody who cares,' Bobby insisted. But somehow no matter which course, no matter who they called or whose door they banged on, there would be Officer Petrie or one of his cronies, probably the Collins look-alike, a couple of those yokels, ending up, at best, arriving, making out their report, dragging Bobby and Lauri off, absolutely ruining the Perkinses' vacation and what would be worse – there was always the possibility that Mrs Hulka would just be sitting inside laughing, sitting next to one of her dolls' houses, or kicking the little dissection kits, alive as can be! *Maybe that's how undertakers get their jollies*, they discussed. And Lauri didn't want her parents involved any more than Bobby wanted his mother and father yanked off Mt Kilgore. Besides, maybe they were wrong, Lauri kept reminding Bobby. Maybe this time it *was* the television or maybe the Hulkas had a perverse sense of humour. 'You know, they love to stage these little scenes in the dolls' houses and maybe they also like staging yellings and things like that, three-D performances to make neighbouring kids think we're losing our minds.'

'That's it, maybe they have a whole thing about entertaining themselves by making believe they kill each other,' Bobby agreed.

'I mean, it's got to get on their brains, don't you think?' Lauri said. 'Burying all those bodies, having that as your occupation, doing nothing but handling corpses day in and day out, and sticking them in their caskets and on displays with all the flowers – ' And then she couldn't go on talking about that any more because she remembered the mass funeral for the Kaminsky family – that day at the church with all the coffins, the different-sized coffins, going into the church, as she managed to make it through the services and made it to the graveyard and the big bouquet of roses that the Geddeses had sent was laid right at the beginning of the path and all the flowers that the whole neighbourhood had donated were at the boundaries by which the mourners walked to the gaping open holes. It had been raining and there was a canvas for everyone to stand under, and there was all the *dust to dust* and the other things ministers say. Lauri had made it all the way through all that, all the way back home from the funeral services, and then she had broken down.

'Who knows what undertakers do?' Bobby intervened. 'You never hear about undertakers winning bridge tournaments or raising prize begonias or being Boy Scout leaders. I never saw a headline that ever said anything like UNDER-

'That *is* strange,' Lauri agreed, moving back to her favourite swivel chair where she could survey the whole heightened clutter of the Perkinses' apartment. For some reason her focus landed on the small butane torch that Mrs Perkins used for her glass and solder sculptures. It was the same kind of torch a chemistry professor she had used to set off a combination of zinc and sulphur that made a cloud like a miniature atom bomb – one of the more spectacular experiments of the academic year at Fort Lee High.

'Mr Hulka probably has to do all the really grisly stuff,' Bobby said, 'and Mrs Hulka probably does the hairdos and make-ups and maybe manicures.' It was then that he noticed the blood was flowing away from Lauri's face again.

'What an emotionally draining job,' Lauri said, fighting an incipient attack.

Bobby put his arm around Lauri. 'Just think of Tahiti,' he reminded her, although he couldn't stop his own mind from thinking about Mrs Hulka leaning over a casket and working her magic with her bottle of White Rain hair-spray. '*This is all in our minds,*' Bobby tried to say as though he believed it. 'We're just projecting, making the whole thing up. It's a big joke.'

'You're right,' Lauri said. Lauri forced herself to laugh, and Bobby tried to laugh along with her. They were both fighting now to change the subject.

'I think we should just go down to McDonald's, have a couple of terrific hamburgers and apple tarts and then go to the aquarium store and watch the kissing gouramies.' He got up and went over to the stereo cabinet and pushed the screwdriver a little farther away from the edge so it wouldn't fall. 'What do you say?' He was about to perk up when he heard the sound of a door opening in the hall. Bobby instinctively yanked open his front door and there was Hulka's door open about six inches, but it quickly

78

slammed. And then he heard all of the Hulkas' three locks snap on.

'Uh-oh,' Bobby whispered to Lauri.

Lauri had heard the sounds. She looked at Bobby. Bobby motioned for her to stay seated and silent while he put the chain lock on his door. Then she watched him wedge a copy of *The Rise and Fall of the Third Reich* so the door would remain open the maximum few inches the chain would permit. But then he moved a heavy wooden chair from the dining-room and slipped it so that it caught under the doorknob. The front door was now firmly ajar. Bobby cleared some electrical junk off a desk chair and lugged it over so that he could sit and see out into the hall. Specifically, he could see a good slice of the hallway which included the Hulkas' door.

'I'll try to smile a lot at McDonald's.' Lauri tried to divert him. 'And then maybe some kids will come over and join us and we'll make some real friends. Real close friends are better than a trip to Tahiti any day.' She swung her long brown hair in forced animation.

'What's one of the problems when you do somebody in?' Bobby enquired.

'Is this a multiple-choice question?' Lauri wanted to know.

'*To get rid of the body*,' Bobby supplied his own answer, his eyes gluing themselves on the Hulkas' door. Lauri was about to say that there are all kinds of things one could do with a body, like stick them in the freezer or a dry-cleaning bag, so there was really no point in keeping watch. If Bobby thought Mr Hulka did have his wife's body in his apartment, there was no need to think he had to dispose of it immediately. 'You can't just sit there and watch his door for ever,' Lauri complained.

'I won't have to,' Bobby said. 'There's a time bomb involved.'

'A bomb!' Lauri exclaimed.

'I'm talking figuratively,' Bobby clarified. 'He's got her

in there. He knows that sooner or later somebody's going to believe us. So he's going to have to get her out of there pretty quick. For all he knows, we've got uncles and aunts with shotguns heading over here right this minute, if not the police.'

Now Lauri found she was getting a little annoyed and that even cheered her up. At least whenever she got annoyed it replaced her nervousness. 'He's not going to just parade the body right by us,' Lauri pointed out. 'What are you expecting? If she's dead, he'll wrap her arm around his shoulder and make believe she's had a few drinks too many . . .' Lauri was going to continue, but then a strange sound began to intrude. The sound was coming from behind the Hulkas' door. This time it didn't have to weave its way through cement or air vents. It just sneaked itself around corners and then slipped from under the Hulkas' door, a sound which Bobby could hear being cushioned by the purple throw rug just behind. It was a mechanical noise, something moving and grinding. The sound of a machine straining. She got up from the sofa and moved next to Bobby at his observation post. It all lasted about a minute and then stopped as suddenly as it had begun.

'What was that?' she asked.

Bobby's face was twitching from side to side as he strained to define the noise. The solution arrived and his facial muscles relaxed. For a moment, his lower jaw fell open. It had been the sound of a luxury item which came as standard equipment only with the most expensive Century Tower apartments. And he knew all the G layouts had one.

'*It's a garbage compacter*,' Bobby said, with meaning.

And now Lauri's eyes, too, were riveted on the Hulkas' door.

Chapter 9

Lauri didn't want to sound too dense but she didn't know exactly how a garbage compacter worked. Unfortunately, Bobby was more than willing to explain that it was smaller than a washing machine but bigger than a bread box and able to squeeze two weeks of garbage into one bag. He was just finished with emphasizing the power of the compacter to crush bones and Coke bottles – when the sound of the machine crawled up to their ears for a second time.

'It can crush anything,' Bobby stated dully. 'Does cycle after cycle until this special bag is filled and it gets all folded up and you stick it out. You have to leave it in the incinerator room for the porters, because it's too big to fit in the regular chute.'

'Oh, I see them on my floor. I was wondering what those bags were.' Lauri began to feel another anxiety attack coming on, so she meandered back to the sofa and stretched out again. She started to hum and this time she did begin to think of palm fronds waving in the wind and coconuts falling – and sucking on sticks of sugar cane. Then the sound of the compacter started in again. 'The Hulkas must have a lot of garbage,' she managed to say between tropical scenes. She felt her heart starting to beat rapidly. If there was one thing she didn't feel like doing, it was hyperventilating, or going into tachycardia or anything complicated like that. So she didn't attempt further speech. She could see Bobby was mesmerized, looking out into the hall, his ears pointed forward, like Mr Spock or some other inhabitant of space. Then she closed her eyes, but her lashes flew open like shutters every time the compacter started in again. There were other sounds now between the sounds of the machine.

Sometimes there were sounds like someone moving about. She could imagine that someone was lugging something. And then sometimes she would hear something that sounded like a slapping sound and a clamour of metal as if someone was rattling through a silverware set or preparing a meal in a kitchen. At another point between grindings there was a type of rapid knocking, like metal upon wood. Maybe it was an onion being chopped, carrots – that's it, Mrs Hulka must be making a stew. That's it, the Hulkas are making dinner. They are both alive and well and they're making dinner. Lauri whispered to Bobby, 'They're making supper and that's why they have a lot of potato skins and beet tops and they have to keep turning on the compacter. They're probably making beef à la mode or something very complicated.' Mrs Hulka was making dinner and maybe Mr Hulka was building a new dolls' house. They had lots of types of houses, but they didn't have a saltbox style, or a really exciting contemporary. Maybe he was working on a contemporary with lots of cantilevered terraces. You have to have lots of tools to build dolls' houses and little wooden people and dinette sets and all those sharp little scalpels and things in the antique dissection kits must really come in handy for a lot of that work. Or maybe they were too valuable to work with. Lauri didn't know anything about that, but the Hulkas were probably just having a normal evening at home. Those sharp little things must be perfect for delicate incisions on balsa wood. Lauri was finally about to actually doze off when she heard the Hulkas' door open. She jumped up off the sofa and this time moved more slowly to Bobby's side, just in time to see Mr Hulka rushing by the Perkinses' door. He didn't even look in. He was just carrying something brown and square, one of those packages she always saw in the incinerator room on the third floor.

'Did you get a good look at his face?' Bobby asked.

'No,' Lauri said, rubbing her eyes.

'He looked stoned,' Bobby said, moving to the hall door

and making certain the dining-room chair was stoutly defending his door from being pushed all the way open. 'His face looked so stoned it could be hanging on Mount Rushmore.' Then came the familiar sound of the incinerator door being opened at the far end of the hall. The door was squeaking as though someone was trying to keep it ajar with a foot, and then ultimately there was the loud slamming. There followed footfalls returning swiftly and eventually the athletic frame of Mr Hulka gracefully hurtling by the Perkinses' door and back into his own apartment. He closed the door and Bobby heard the one, two, three clicking of the locks.

'What's that all about?' Lauri wanted to know.

'Don't ask.'

'I want to know.'

'No, you don't.'

'Yes, I do.'

'You'll only turn white again.'

'I won't,' Lauri said. 'In fact, if you don't tell me I'll turn red. I'm getting very angry. It's only my legs that want to fall down.'

Bobby spoke coldly, almost scientifically. 'I think Mrs Hulka has just been put out as garbage.'

'Oh,' Lauri said. 'Oh,' she repeated, and then started to whistle. She started playing with her hair and looking out the window and jerking her head a little awkwardly. And this time she could feel her red corpuscles galloping for her fingertips. She didn't want Bobby to see she was zombie white, so she rearranged her hair to cover most of her face. She didn't have the best peripheral vision in the world as it was, but the attempt to hide behind hair had always been one of her standard manœuvres.

She glanced at Bobby long enough to see that he was thinking very hard. She managed to make it back to the sofa and this time she began chewing on the entire lemon wedge, pips and all. Bobby cleared his voice, ready with a report. 'We know he wasn't in that incinerator room long enough to break that bag into enough pieces to ram down the small chute. So that means he just left it in there. It'll just sit there until one of the porters comes up in the service elevator and takes it out along with all the rest of the Glad bags that don't make it into the chute. Then before you know it they'll just send it out on a truck. It'll be on a barge, burning, and they'll dump it, and that'll be the end of the evidence. He'll get away with the whole thing. *You wait here*,' he ordered, pulling the dining-room chair away from the doorknob.

'I don't want to wait here. He might jump around the terrace.'

'The terrace door is locked; I checked it.'

'He'll break through the glass.'

'That's double Thermopane. A bullet couldn't get through that glass.'

Lauri grabbed Bobby's hand as he prepared to release the door chain. 'For all we know Hulka could be on patrol behind his door, looking out his peephole, and as soon as you go out in the hall, then he'll just come right after you.'

'That's what I'm talking about,' Bobby said. 'That's why you've got to stay. If he comes running out at least you'll be in here and we won't *both* end up like Mrs Hulka.'

'Why not?' Lauri said. 'He'll kill you in the hall or the incinerator room and then he'll come back and get me. I'll be on the phone yelling – but who's going to believe me? You've heard the story of The Boy Who Cried Wolf? Well, the same thing goes for rabbit fur!'

'Just do as I'm telling you,' Bobby commanded.

'No,' Lauri insisted. 'We'll call the police. Call Officer Petrie and tell him we don't want to go over his head.'

'And then what?'

'Tell him the truth.'

'What? That a man changed his wife into a bag of refuse? Nosirree.'

'Yes,' Lauri insisted.

Bobby began to jump about anxiously. 'I'm telling you, Lauri, I'm going to zip out and you put the chain back on, and if Hulka charges down the hall while I'm in the incinerator room, all you have to do is scream and keep screaming.'

'He'll get you,' Lauri protested. 'He'll get you and he'll get me.'

'As long as you scream I'll have enough time to lie down on the floor in the incinerator room and stick my feet up against the door. Either that or I could split out and run down the exit stairs.'

'Twenty-three flights?'

'Sure. Hulka thinks he's young, but I'll tell you, I'm a lot faster.'

'No,' Lauri said. 'Crazy men run very fast. Besides, baby Jesus, I think they were just cooking dinner in there. That's what all the noises were. They just stuck their dinner out there.'

'Oh, sure,' Bobby said, throwing up his hands. 'Mrs Hulka lets out a scream and then goes and cooks dinner.' Bobby suddenly stopped his dancing about and lifted Lauri's chin. He looked at her closely and could see she was in pretty good shape now that there was a real adventure going on. 'Can you run if you have to?'

'You bet I can,' Lauri insisted.

'All right. Man the battle stations and get ready to go over the top.'

Bobby made sure the dining-room chair wouldn't block the front door when he swung it open. He checked the door to make certain it would lock when he slammed it. He also checked his left pocket to make sure he had his keys. 'Keys and money,' he said out loud. His hand was shaking slightly as he lifted the chain latch free. Lauri would flee first and he would bring up the rear. If they could make it to the incinerator room they could summon the service elevator. It was too risky to try to use the regular elevator in the hall.

'*Now*,' Bobby shouted.

As fast as weasels Lauri and Bobby traversed the long hallway towards the incinerator room. Lauri got about fifty feet and then fell flat on her face because she was too busy looking behind her. Bobby fell down on top of her and in a flash they were on their feet again. A few seconds later they jumped into the incinerator room. Bobby yelled, 'Press the elevator button,' as he sprawled flat out on the floor, his feet against the inside of the door and his hands stiff against the far wall just beneath the small metal door through which ordinary-size junk was disposed of. There on the floor was the compacter bag, all neat and waterproof, sealed like an artistic product from a Chinese laundry. It looked too beautiful with its trimmed edges and squared corners to be garbage, but it was. Garbage and then some, Bobby thought to himself.

Lauri kept banging on the elevator button, pushing it this way and that way, praying that it wasn't broken. Only ten seconds went by, but it seemed like an hour as Lauri practically jumped up and down, watching the illuminated dial read out that the elevator was now at floor number seventeen, eighteen, nineteen . . . She began repeating a rhyme to herself, *nine, ten, a big fat hen*. The elevator was almost there and still there was no Mr Hulka trying to break in on them. There was no giant pounding on the outside door, no face peering in through the glass with the wire webbing. She accepted the opening of the elevator doors as a miracle and jumped inside, slamming her hand against the HOLD button. In a flash, Bobby was off the floor and if Hulka was going to get them, it would be in the next crucial moment. Bobby strained to pick up the compacter bag, and was shocked at its weight. Whatever was in it was at least a hundred pounds, he thought. Then he was in the elevator and the doors were closing and finally they were safe. They were mechanically heading downward towards the lobby and civilization.

'Is she in there?' Lauri asked, pointing at the bag.

'It's pretty heavy,' Bobby observed. 'It might be everything except her head or a leg.' When he had already said that, he wanted to bite off his tongue, because he could see Lauri ready to slide down the wall of the elevator.

'It's probably just garbage,' he added quickly. 'Just garbage and we probably made a big mistake and we'll just forget about it, but I'll just look anyway.' He ripped open the top of the container and there was a sudden squirt of red fluid splashing his right knuckles.

'Don't look,' Bobby gasped, but it was too late. Lauri was sinking, and sinking fast, holding on to the buttons of the elevator. He caught her just as she was dwindling below ordinary gravitational stability, and shook her. He tried pinching her cheeks to keep her conscious, but some of the sticky red fluid inadvertently got on her face. She lifted up her hand and touched it, and then looked disbelievingly at the stain. The whole mess had gone beyond the point of giving her an anxiety attack, and now she was becoming outraged. *How dare any man kill anyone*, she said to herself. *How dare anyone kill any living thing!* She felt a sense of reverse peristalsis starting in. When the elevator doors flew open at the far left of the lobby, a breath of fresh air rushed in and brought her around. They were in the corner where all the service-related ingresses and egresses occurred at the Century Tower, anything that would shame the glamour of the fancy Century Tower Apartments lobby. Lauri was the first to see Joe the Schmo as she stumbled out and began to gain speed. She ran towards him yelling, 'Help! Help!'

Joe the Schmo turned, and when he saw the sight of Lauri and Bobby scurrying towards him, a scowl festered on his face. After the scowl came a grimace of disbelief as he zeroed in on Bobby hobbling with a garbage bag. A few tenants were near the front door – including an old lady with little streaked ringlets and a white sheepdog in a summer clip. Two rather distinguished-looking men were picking up their mail from the concierge's desk and chatting about an upcoming weekend on Shelter Island. A child stopped bouncing a ball near a statue of Venus which was the pièce de résistance of the Italian rococo decorations. Bobby felt the red fluid flowing over his hands, pouring out of the top of the bag as though from a wound. He couldn't carry it much farther. He would get it to Joe, then Joe would see, Joe would have to believe, and then Joe would call the police and everything would be all right. Everyone would know what was true. Lauri had already reached Joe and was babbling a mile a minute and Bobby could see Joe the Schmo was looking angrier and angrier and he had every right to be, Bobby believed, because it was all too preposterous. He knew the red fluid was now flowing on the carpet and then on the black marble floor and, finally, Bobby could hold it no longer and he let the bag drop. It crashed down on to the hard surface, bursting, and there it was, its contents spilled for all to see.

'It's Mrs Hulka!' Bobby screamed, pointing to the mess on the floor. He was afraid to examine the fragments too closely with his eyes, the compressed mass, the sectioned heap. Instead he looked at Joe's face and then at Lauri who hadn't passed out at all. In fact, all she looked was a little puzzled.

'*This* is Mrs Hulka?' Joe the Schmo enquired measuredly.

Bobby looked down and there was a heap of crushed milk cartons, old broccoli stalks, wrinkled tin cans, orange rinds, coffee grounds, pieces of wood, and on top of the whole mishmash lay the glass remnants of what must have once been a full bottle of Heinz ketchup.

Bobby looked at Lauri.

Lauri looked at Bobby.

They both looked at Joe the Schmo.

'My error,' Bobby said calmly, grabbing up as much of the mess as his arms could hold. He signalled Lauri with a swing of his head and they both ran back towards the service elevator while Joe the Schmo began to make sounds like an enraged fruit peddler whose cart had just been knocked over.

'Press three,' Bobby yelped, jumping in.

Lauri tapped fast and hard and even tried to help the elevator doors close, shutting out the boiling scene in the lobby. Bobby stepped quickly to the rear and opened his arms, letting the mess he was clutching fall into a corner. 'He tricked us,' Bobby said, bubbling with anger. 'He tricked us.'

'Who?'

'*Hulka!* Nobody throws a full bottle of ketchup into a compacter.'

'I don't care how many bottles of ketchup he throws in, just so long as he doesn't throw his wife in,' Lauri added, thankful that it had been a wild-goose chase. Just one more incredible adventure, but Bobby had really gone rather far this time. The elevator doors opened on the third-floor incinerator room. Lauri got out first and opened the door to the hallway and Bobby came out brushing coffee grounds off his hips and arms. His hands were still wet and red. 'Hurry,' he said, dashing towards Lauri's apartment. 'Get your keys and open up.'

Lauri fumbled, finally found the keys, and got the door open. Bobby ran for the kitchen sink, shooting orders all the while. 'Call the garage,' he insisted, rubbing his hands under the stream of aerated water.

'Mom,' Lauri called out, a bit dazed from all the demands. 'Mom, are you home?' She wasn't.

Lauri heard Bobby still shooting off his mouth. He was talking like they were still in the middle of some kind of race. 'I said *call the garage!*'

'Why?'

'I'll explain as soon as I get this goo off me.'

'Bobby, look, let's admit we made a mistake.'

'We did not.' Bobby hurried by her, drying his hands on a dish towel and yanking the receiver to the in-house phone off its hook. He dialled the garage and balanced the receiver between his jaw and left shoulder, while he continued wiping off his clothes.

'What?' he heard Rucci's scratchy voice on the phone. He could just picture Rucci down in the garage booth, really angry at being interrupted from reading a comic book.

'Have you seen Mr Hulka from apartment twenty-four-G?' Bobby asked, using a slightly British accent.

'Who wants to know?' came the retort, echoing in a manner which meant Rucci had probably opened the booth door and was peering out to check the A level of the garage. '*His nephew*,' Bobby lied.

'Yeah.'

'Yeah *what*?'

'I seen Mr Hulka,' Rucci clarified.

'Where?'

'I think he's on level C.'

'Was he carrying anything?'

'A suitcase,' Rucci garbled, as though it was taxing his brain to remember the electronic image he had seen.

'Big or small?' Bobby wanted to know.

'What is this, twenty questions?'

'Hey, you just tell me, was it big or small, or I'm going to report you to the concierge,' Bobby threatened, forgetting to maintain his English accent.

'*Big*,' Rucci complied. 'Hey, who is this?' he added, getting a little suspicious at last.

'Attila the Hun,' Bobby said, and hung up. In a flash he was galloping for the Geddeses' front door.

'Where are you going?' Lauri cried out.

'Tell you later,' Bobby called over his shoulder, disappearing into the hall.

'Do you want me to come with you?' she bellowed, but he was already gone. Lauri felt like a mouse standing in front of a maze. She didn't know what to do, and it took her a full five seconds to make up her mind. She went running back out the door, slamming it behind her. She was getting so much exercise she was beginning to feel like she was overprogrammed in gym. She made it into the hall just in time to see Bobby disappearing down the exit stairs. She was after him. No longer any time to be frightened, just insatiably curious. It didn't take much for her to catch up with him because he had a lot of obstacles. He had to open several doors, including the heavy exit door, to reach the lobby. She gained more ground as he had to fake out Joe the Schmo as though he were trying to make a goal in a football game. The commotion in the lobby was building. Joe the Schmo was harshly protesting. A few more ladies with canines were flitting this way and that. The dogs were all rather fascinated by the aroma of the remains of the garbage which was still lying limply in the middle of the lobby floor.

Bobby jumped into the revolving door, and a second later Lauri was doing a revolution of her own. Outside, Bobby stopped short under the entrance canopy when Lauri caught him. He was frozen, staring across the green oval. A familiar cranking sound floated towards them. Lauri saw the huge garage door mechanically lifting up, opening like a mouth, and a black station-wagon with dark tinted windows came roaring out. It accelerated with such abandonment it seemed as though it was going to smack right into the side of a bright yellow Checker cab that had made the mistake of pulling into the oval at exactly the moment the garage door had yawned open.

To the left of the garage, in a booth, was Rucci, braying over the loudspeakers for the cars to halt, but there wasn't time for that. Instead, the driver of the station-wagon peeled rubber and spun several feet with a noise that alerted the cab driver. The cab driver hit his brakes while the station-wagon swung clear and began to complete the large circle, bringing it by the pillars of the front entrance. It was heading straight for Lauri and Bobby as though it would leap the kerb and deliberately run them down. But then, it jerked again, and Mr Hulka's face could be glimpsed for just a moment behind the dyed glass.

The station-wagon shot off the Century Tower grounds as a rather befuddled cab driver stepped out and said, 'Hey, what's going on?'

A man with a cane got out of the cab, threw some money at the cab driver and went muttering under the canopy, heading for the building.

'Follow that car,' Bobby yelled at the cab driver, jumping in the back seat.

'I will not,' the cab driver said.

Bobby tried to think inventively. What would his father do at such a moment? He'd be practical. 'There's an extra ten bucks in it if you do,' Bobby stated.

Lauri stayed on the edge of the kerb until she saw that Bobby had indeed pronounced the magic words. The cab driver was back behind the wheel in a flash.

'Wait for me,' she cried out, and then pounced in the back seat next to Bobby. She hardly had a chance to shut the door before the cab jumped forward like a bright gaudy canary, and the last thing she saw parenthesized in the rear window was Joe the Schmo pounding his chest in rage, drooling like a dragon that had just lost its prey.

Chapter 10

Bobby got into an argument with the cab driver because he wanted the ten-dollar tip before they even reached Main Street. Bobby grunted but gave 'him the cash, only after insisting that he run a red light so that Hulka's station-wagon wouldn't get out of sight.

'You're corrupt,' Bobby told the cab driver.

'So what?' the cab driver said.

Lauri whispered into Bobby's ear, while holding on to a hand strap for all she was worth. 'Maybe if you told him why we've got to follow the station-wagon, he'd understand.'

Bobby sank back in the rear seat and deliberately braced his feet on the jump-seat. 'He wouldn't believe us,' Bobby explained. 'This is the kind of cab driver who aims for squirrels.'

After only about five minutes, the cab driver wanted another advance on the meter, so Bobby threw his last five-dollar bill at him.

'Here. Just don't lose that guy.' A few minutes later they were roaring down the hill past the point where Fort Lee becomes Leonia.

'You lost him, didn't you?' Bobby said.

'No,' the driver growled.

'If he loses him, he loses him,' Lauri tried to comfort Bobby. 'Besides, what do we do if he catches him?'

Suddenly the driver jammed on the brakes.

'He's getting away.' Bobby sat forward, banging on the driver partition, seeing that the station-wagon had made a sharp left turn.

'He's not getting anywhere,' the cab driver said. 'That's a dead-end street.'

'Dead end?' Lauri repeated automatically.

'Yeah,' the cabbie said, 'and don't worry, I'll keep the change.'

'Look,' Bobby said, leaning over the front seat, 'that was a maniac driving that car.'

'Who isn't?' the cab driver commented.

Bobby really told the cabbie off every second during the disembarking, calling him a bad citizen, a blight on the American economic system, and a ruthless capitalist.

'Supply and demand,' the cabbie said.

Lauri slithered out of the back seat and was simply resigned to the fact that the adventure was going on. She was thankful they were only in Leonia, which was less than a mile from the centre of Fort Lee. They could walk home from here if they had to.

'If you read in tomorrow's papers,' Bobby presented to the cab driver as his final words, 'that two kids who look like us are missing, just tell the cops where you let us off. That's the least you can do.'

'You're nuts,' the driver said, and the Checker took off in a flash of yellow, stirring up some fallen leaves in the gutter.

Lauri could tell Bobby was looking to her for a reaction. 'I didn't want you to come along. I could have handled this myself,' he said.

'Nonsense,' Lauri assured him. 'It's a lovely neighbourhood. Besides, I've always wanted to go down Main Street at seventy miles an hour.'

Bobby sniffed the air like a bloodhound. The street was tree-lined, a lot of shrubbery, with most of the houses set way back, practically out of view. Expensive homes, clusters of thick rhododendrons. He could smell the wealth and it made him even more curious about where Mr Hulka had gone. He walked to the corner with Lauri following him. Lauri knew he wasn't in the mood for conversation. He was thinking too hard, processing information, exploring. Lauri hoped the dead-end street would be fifty miles long, because then it would be practically impossible to find the station-wagon, and then they could just go home

94

and have a nice quiet late-afternoon tea and a big bowl of Fritos. Unfortunately, the street turned out to be the shortest dead-end street Lauri had ever seen. In fact, it was more like an indentation, a recess from the road where Good Humor trucks could park. A street sign announced, Elm Place, and from the looks of it, Elm Place boasted only a single home of rather vast proportions. Not a Spanish sort of mansion like movie stars live in in California, but this was definitely one of the largest, most opulent homes Lauri had ever seen. The landscaping was lush, old and comfortable, ivy crawling up the brick. There seemed to be two or three empty lots on the right side, approaching the house, wooded acreage on which other large houses could be built, which was probably how this minute thoroughfare was able to deserve a name at all. The landscaping of the mansion was lush, ivy crawling up the brick sides, trying to strangle the several chimneys. It was right out of a magazine, Lauri decided. Summer flowers in bloom, the driveway lined with weeping willows, and all of Lauri's most favourite trees, including a monstrous red maple. The only thing that threw a damper on the entire façade was a large ornately lettered sign which proclaimed, *Hulka's Funeral Home.*

Bobby flipped his hand into Lauri's and pulled her into a break in the line of ancient hedges, great tall bushes with leaf-crowded branches, all reaching upward like fat fingers towards the darkening sky. These hedges ran the entire length of the left-hand side of the driveway. He motioned her not to speak, and then leaned out far enough to see that the station-wagon had parked on the extreme left side of the house, near an ugly large brick annexe, which had no doubt been built behind the mansion like some sort of architectural desecration. It was as offensive and cheap looking as the elephant end tables.

Mr Hulka had parked right outside the rear door of the annexe, which was a good distance from where Bobby and Lauri stood. He was checking all the doors of the station-wagon to make certain they were locked. He double-checked the rear-panel door, and then disappeared into the annexe.

At that moment an enormously long silver-grey Cadillac hearse came pulling off the main road and drove right by the spot where Bobby and Lauri were hiding behind the hedge. The driver looked rather young, sporting a long nose and a chauffeur's uniform. The hearse had *Hulka* tastefully inscribed, grey on grey, on the door. Lauri and Bobby strained to look through the hedges to watch the car swinging around the driveway to the right side of the house, walking under a breezeway supported by enormous columns. The man with the long nose got out and strode like a swift regal heir into a side entrance which looked like it housed the main office of Hulka's Funeral Home.

Bobby sat down on a small mound of grass which reached its way up to cover the root of one of the giant hedges. By leaning low enough he could see through the thick beginnings of the bush without being seen. Lauri sat down next to him.

'Bobby,' she said, 'I don't want you to think it hasn't been fun, but how about going home? It's getting dark.'

Bobby looked upward for a moment and realized she was right. It was getting dark and a little cool. 'Good,' Bobby said, returning his attention to the house.

'Good *what*?' Lauri asked.

'That it's getting dark.'

Lauri manœuvred a finger to slide a pebble out from the side of one of her shoes. She rubbed her eyes and decided to at least be grateful that things were quieting down for a while. This was all a little bit like having a picnic, a picnic at dusk. It sounded almost romantic.

'At least tell me what's going on. I lost track at the ketchup,' Lauri begged.

'Hulka knows *we* know he killed his wife.'

'I don't know that.'

'I do.'

'Well, I still don't,' Lauri said. 'In fact, you know, if

we left right now we could still walk to McDonald's and get a table.'

Bobby looked her straight in the eye. His face was serious. His eyes an extra dark shade of green. 'I think it's better, anyway, that you think the screams came from the television, or a little marital squabble. In fact, I want you to go home. I wanted you to be home safe in your apartment. I didn't want you to run out the front door and jump in the cab.' He gave her a gentle hug. 'I'll call you after I check it out.'

'Check what out?'

'Something.'

Lauri groaned. 'Now, Bobby, you tell me what you're talking about.'

'If I tell you, will you go home?'

'If you really want me to.'

'You promise?'

'Cross my heart and hope to die,' Lauri said quickly, and then realized maybe she hadn't used quite the right expression.

The shadows were beginning to change the elegance of the grounds into something less inviting. Bobby decided he better tell her what he thought was going on. 'Hulka knew we were watching his door, so he faked us out.'

'I never thought of that.'

'Of course, I didn't know exactly what he was going to do. Sometimes people who kill their wives cement them right into the shower stalls and walls and all kinds of places. This guy is too smart. He's crazy, but smart. While we were sidetracked with the compacter bag, he put poor Mrs Hulka in a suitcase.'

Lauri looked towards the house. She remembered Mr Hulka checking the back door of the station-wagon, making doubly sure that it was locked.

'Sometimes people move books in suitcases,' Lauri said. 'Lot of things. Sometimes they go on trips.'

'Not this time,' Bobby insisted. 'Hulka's got her in a nice large piece of Samsonite, or a Saks Fifth Avenue trunk, or something, and that Pinocchio chauffeur is probably also the caretaker who sleeps here, and maybe helps with the embalming or something, the resident slave. But he probably doesn't know anything about what's going on.'

'Then why would Hulka risk driving over here?'

'Well, he's got the car locked. So maybe Long-nose wasn't even supposed to be here. Maybe he was just due in from a small-time funeral in Paterson.'

Lauri didn't want to ruin Bobby's flight of fancy, but she couldn't let all this go on much longer. Her mother would be home by now and soon she'd wonder where they were. Lauri also knew they were going to have fettucini Alfredo, with escarole fried in olive oil. 'If it was a funeral, then where's the flower car?' Lauri asked.

'So maybe it wasn't a funeral,' Bobby said, as he pointed to the far back of the grounds where the driveway branched wide and led to a huge garage, which looked like it could hold half the fleet of the sanitation department. 'Maybe Long-nose went out for milk, or a loaf of bread. The point I'm making is that Hulka brought the suitcase here because he's going to do something to it. He's got to do something with Mrs Hulka. Maybe he'll give Long-nose the night off, get him out, then embalm her and stick her in a closed coffin and put it smack on display in one of the parlours and tell Long-nose it's a new arrival, and the family wanted a closed coffin.'

'Wouldn't Long-nose think it was strange?' Lauri questioned. 'Nobody would come to pay respects?'

'Nah,' Bobby stated. 'I think any undertaker in this country could bury his wife without anyone noticing she's gone. I don't think anybody would ever miss an undertaker's wife. He could just bury her under another name. He probably even sells plots on the side. Maybe even owns a whole cemetery and he does mail-order business. Who knows?'

Bobby and Lauri sat very still as lights began to go on inside the funeral parlour. Suddenly the large sign in front was also illuminated. The bushes, trees, and the fountain, all cuddling the mansion, lit up, making it look a little like a Miami Beach hotel.

'How pretty,' Lauri observed.

Bobby looked at Lauri. 'Look, I've got to know what you're feeling inside. What's going on in your head. You know I always used to do that with you, no matter how wild any adventure was. I've got to know what you're feeling like.'

Lauri felt very much like giving him a kiss when he said that, but she didn't dare. Holding hands, taking his arm, giving hugs, that was all permissible. It was strange, she had often mused to herself, no matter how modern and swinging everybody made believe they were, there still didn't seem to be any replacement for real emotion. In fact, she was beginning to believe that *emotion* was the fundamental building block of life. She didn't know exactly how she was coming to this belief. The only thing she felt was that it was closely connected to the fact that she felt very old. No matter how young she really was in years, you feel old at any age when Death is stalking you. Her fear of Death had made her desperate to touch and be close to another human being.

'I'm okay,' she said.

'Can you make it home alone?' Bobby asked, searching his pockets to see if he had a few singles left. 'You could just knock on somebody's door and tell them to call a cab.'

'What are you going to do?' Lauri wanted to know.

'I just want to get a closer look,' Bobby said.

But Lauri could sense that was an understatement if she ever heard one.

'You shouldn't,' Lauri said.

'You promised,' Bobby reminded her, pressing some money into her hand.

'Oh,' Lauri sighed. She was very uncomfortable now, just lying on the mound. She felt like a bunch of ants were going to come along and absolutely just ruin the picnic.

Besides, it was still only a game, but it *was* getting late.

'You *promised*,' Bobby reiterated.

'Why do you need to be miserable?' she asked. 'Why do you always want to get in trouble?'

'Lauri, please go home. If I don't call or come back within an hour, just tell your mother to call the police, and let them know my life's been snuffed out in a Leonia funeral parlour. It's no big deal. Please, *honey*?'

Lauri perked up at the fact that he had actually called her 'honey'. It was as if it had just slipped out naturally.

'Bobby,' Lauri said, 'it's your old Jack-and-the-Beanstalk syndrome. I think it's one of the problems you have socially, too. Sometimes you act as though you're always waiting for somebody to spray Black Flag on your Pop-Tarts, or that some mad shootist is going to break out of the penitentiary in Denver and Lady Luck will have you in the crowd when he attacks.'

'That's not true,' Bobby said. 'I just do think there's a lot of mean people in this world, and they shouldn't get away with it. And Hulka's not going to get away with this.'

His head was silhouetted against the backdrop of the funeral home, and Lauri could barely distinguish his features, it had got so dark. 'Bobby, we sort of know why *I'm* afraid to die. We never really talk about you. We just always sort of laugh that off. And I don't think I've been very much of a friend to you because up to now I've been too scared to talk about it, but I think you've finally driven me to it.'

'Well, we don't have time to talk about it now,' Bobby protested, standing up and brushing off the seat of his pants.

Lauri got up and she grabbed his arm this time. 'You've done so much for me. You got me to be able to sit around a campfire out on the cliffs and roast marshmallows and frankfurters. I don't break out into a cold sweat when someone lights a cigarette. I don't mind it when your mother turns on the stove and I have to look at jets of gas. I can even do it now myself. I know you've done everything possible to make me unafraid of fire, and everything else. But you keep doing things that get you into a lot of trouble. They don't yell at me so much. It's you they take it out on. Couldn't we just both go, have a hamburger and talk about it? It's going a little too far this time, the adventure,' Lauri pleaded.

'You promised,' Bobby said, unyieldingly.

Lauri thought a moment. She kicked her foot in the dirt; it really was starting to feel cold. She didn't want to tell him because he would give her his shirt, and he'd catch a cold. And she was getting hungry. She could just smell all the delicious things simmering and bubbling in her mother's kitchen. 'All right,' she said, deciding that the worst thing that could possibly happen was that the police would bring him home in a patrol car for molesting a mortuary. 'I'll go home, but if you're not back in an hour, then I will call the police.'

'You won't be frightened going home alone?' Bobby asked, as if he was beginning to soften in his demand. 'You won't think a seagull is going to fly over your head and drop a clam, or anything like that?'

'No,' Lauri said, now feeling as though she was challenged to show she had enough nerve to make it home alone. 'In fact, I wanted to tell you for some time that lately I'm not very frightened about me at all. I'm more frightened for you. I just care about you.' She started walking away, but then turned. 'One hour,' she stressed.

'You bet.'

Lauri scooted quickly on to the main street, and then she was out of Bobby's sight.

Bobby counted to a hundred slowly before he made his first move. Leaves and branches broke beneath his feet as he started the trek. Small spaces opened up in the hedges from point to point and he could see glimpses of more and more detail of the house the nearer he got. Halfway there, he was relieved because he could actually see Mr Hulka and Long-nose in the brightly lit office to the far right of the mansion. Bobby speculated that Hulka was probably making a lot of excuses about why he was there, or thinking of ways to keep the chauffeur away from the left side of the house. Between those two polarities of the funeral home had to be all the viewing rooms where visitors could come to pay respects to the dead. The funeral parlour looked large enough to handle five or six separate requiems at a time, and the middle rooms were mostly dark. A lit doorway or shrub here or there allowed some light to reveal rows of chairs inside a few of the rooms. In one room, to the left of the centre entrance, Bobby was certain he could see a coffin, and when he got a little closer, he could even see the sprays of flowers displayed, showing a rather massive expression of sympathy for someone who was obviously quite breathless and reclining inside the closed coffin. Maybe viewing hours would be from eight to ten o'clock. Maybe that was it. Long-nose would probably have to conduct the viewing hours for this departed one, a sort of macabre maître d', seeing that all the mourners signed the guest book and knew where to hang up their coats or hats.

Finally, he reached the far rear corner of the house. He was behind the hedges, right where the station-wagon was parked, and if he stepped out now he would risk being seen, if anyone was about. As long as Mr Hulka stayed at the other end of the house, he really didn't have to worry, unless there were some other workmen around. Bobby took a final check to make certain Mr Hulka was still in the office, and then dashed out of the hedges, past the station-wagon. He didn't have to stop to see the suitcase; it was inside behind the shadowed glass. In a flash, he was inside the annexe, and what he saw made his entire head bristle as though he had been hooked up to a Van de Graaff generator. He was in the casket showroom. There were about thirty different kinds of caskets, all lined up and presented like products in a supermarket. Each one was like an exhibit, with a price clearly visible near the base. Some were on low platforms; some were on high platforms. It looked more like a setting for a quiz show where contestants could run up and down various levels and pick out a prize. They were made of all sorts of materials: deep dark mahogany, with bronze metal hooks and handles; some were all metallic and looked like the hoods of medium-priced cars; and one startling expensive coffin looked like it was made of pure silver, glistening on the highest pedestal. It was the Rolls-Royce of caskets, Bobby thought. Not only would worms have a hard time getting in, but it would really make it hard for *dust to dust* to have much meaning. All of those oblong boxes, with the front of the tops lifted up like Dutch doors to reveal a variety of plush insides and linings which ran the gamut from taffeta to embossed velvet. The room was lit so prettily, as though Bobby had stumbled into the inside of a Christmas tree. The only really bright light was over a sign near the door which had fancy lettering and which proudly announced, 'Price includes all funeral services.' Bobby moved quickly down the aisles, zigzagging, looking for any clue. He was deep into the showroom, too deep, when he heard the footsteps; the footsteps and a man whistling. Someone was coming from the domain of the greater house.

Chapter 11

Lauri didn't get a block away before she had the distinct feeling that a giant hawk was going to swoop out of the trees, sink its talons into her hair, and lift her up into the sky. It was just a passing thought, and she decided she would rather make up one of her imaginary letters to Bobby. That would be more soothing for the walk home. Maybe she'd even write it all down when she got home, and actually deliver it, turn it over to him the moment he got back. She decided she'd begin the letter very directly and simply say, *Dear Bobby*, and then she'd go on and she'd say, *As I'm walking home leaving you at the funeral parlour, I know I'm losing physical contact with you, but spiritually I know we're still together. I don't believe Mr Hulka killed Mrs Hulka, but if it gets you to call me 'honey' I'll go along with anything. I've been wanting to write you this letter for months, and it would have been so personal it would have embarrassed you, that's how badly I wanted to confess my feelings to you. You would have turned red and given up on me, and I'd be totally alone now, in every way.*

I am alone now, Lauri thought to herself, as she slowed down her pace along the main street. She could see the hill starting to rise ahead of her, leading from Leonia back into Fort Lee. She turned around half expecting to see that Bobby would be walking right behind her. She had even seen a shadow but she decided that it was only some large summer moth fluttering under a streetlight. She stopped under the light and decided maybe it would be better if she just waited five or ten minutes to see if Bobby might not be along. A couple of cars passed by, but she didn't pay any attention to them. She decided to go on thinking about the letter she would write if she had a pad and pencil. She'd sit right down and she'd write it then and there, and she'd say, *Oh, Bobby, I wanted so much for you to know that there is a chip of ice in my heart that is starting to melt because of you. If there is a God in this world, I don't know why he did that terrible thing to my neighbours in Edison, and I don't know why he made my blood run cold with fear. But what I do know is that you're very dear to me because you're making me remember what it's like for me to have feelings of love again. I never told you this, but I had a crush on the Kaminsky boy, who tried to cook himself a steak, but then ended up burning himself and his family to death. He never knew it, any more than you know now how I feel about you, but I've decided that at last I have enough nerve to tell you. I hope that you don't mind that I'm writing this, but I can't speak about it yet. I just can't say the words to you face to face, so you'll have to fill in all the tones of deep emotion that are before you in these simple words on my meagre paper. Oh, Bobby, I feel as though I am involved in a bizarre ménage à trois. You know, a ménage à trois is when you have three people all linked to each other, like in a love triangle, but in this case, it seems as though the triangle consists of you, me and the third character is Death.*

Lauri's mind went blank for a moment. She didn't know how she would continue the letter. It was getting to be a real downer, and she hoped that if she ever really did write it that Bobby wouldn't think that she was trying to be too fancy with a French expression. Lauri strained to see if there was any motion from behind her, anything moving at all down the street, but there wasn't. She felt a pain in her right index finger, and lifted it up to see that a mosquito was brazenly penetrating her skin with its nasal hypodermic. She gave it a quick slap, leaving a residue of splashed scarlet and a few mangled legs.

'Ugh,' she said aloud as she grabbed out a Kleenex and wiped her finger clean. And then for some reason she had this crazy thought, that maybe Mr Hulka was a vampire.

Now that's truly a dumb thought, she told herself. So she laughed out loud and then cut her laugh short as a real bat made a dip under the streetlight. It was just an average little New Jersey night bat, she knew, and then she started to walk on towards Leonia Avenue. From there it would be only about three-quarters of a mile – all uphill, of course – but there'd be the McDonald's stand, and she could get a cup of coffee, and then Bobby would be back, and they could have a big laugh about the whole thing. *Oh, Bobby, you're so funny, I love you.* That's what she'd say in the letter. She'd have to really stress how much she adored his sense of humour and his sense of ethics. *Some day you're going to be the most popular kid in school. Some day you're going to be the most popular person on earth. The world is waiting for an injection of truth, and you're going to give it to it.* She'd really stress how much she adored Bobby's humour. She'd write, *I mean, the details you gave everyone about how you saw Mr Hulka wrestling with this bundle of white fur and the legs hanging out, with the shoes, and Mr Hulka carrying the heap into the bedroom. You probably even knew Mrs Hulka had gone out that morning and that she'd be coming back any minute, and I know you cooked it all up for my sake.* No – she wouldn't write that. She could sense it wasn't *all* made up just for her but she couldn't deal with that so she returned to her own imagination. *And, Bobby, oh, Bobby, please forget everything else I've said in this letter and just let me come right out with it and tell you that I want our friendship to change. I'm ready for it now, Bobby. I really am. At least, I'm almost ready, I think. I love you, Bobby, and I want us to be together in friendship and in love, and I'm writing this to you because it's the most important thing that has ever happened in my life. I see only you when I close my eyes. I have dreams about you saving me when I am in an arena and a vicious lion is about to attack me. You're always my saviour, and to me you're very handsome. You're handsome and mysterious and kind,*

*and even if you've only taken me on as an emotional
charity case, please try to think of me as something more.*
Lauri could feel another thought intruding upon her. 'This
was not all a big prank,' the thought said, but she pushed
the little voice back under a fold in her brain. *Whenever
I'm not with you I feel disembodied. I need you next to
me. I miss you now, here on the street, walking. I need
to be with you while you're reading this, so if you want
to tell me I have no right to tell you my real feelings, you
can do it. I wouldn't blame you if you hated me. I've
always left everything up to you, but I can't do that much
longer. I've got to tell you who is really hiding here inside
of me. It's someone who cherishes you, who wants to be
held by you, who wants to hold you in return. I want our
souls to know each other. I want our hopes and dreams
to collide together, to become one as though two great
planets met in the galaxies. I want to be so close to you,
anything God or Nature sends against us will never destroy
us, only test us. I believe there are electrons flying around
the outside of our bodies which are combining, linking,
making us more and more into one. I know this may all
be my own selfish fantasy, but I can't keep it to myself
any longer.*

Suddenly, Lauri stopped in her tracks. She decided she
had better give herself a lecture. She looked behind, but
still no one was coming. Who are you kidding? she told
herself. You'll never write that letter. Here you are making
up this whole hearts-and-flowers spiel about how much you
love Bobby and then you just walk off and leave him to
get in trouble. She knew he was just doing the whole thing
for her, and she was letting him get too involved. She
didn't protest enough. She could have dragged him out of
there if she really made a big fuss. If she really had any
feelings about him at all, she should just turn right around
and march back there. 'Come out of those hedges, Bobby,'
is what she should have said. 'We have bigger fish to fry.'
That was a great expression. *We need to be really honest*

with each other. I don't want you arrested for trespassing. But I wanted to just tell you that I want to rest my head next to your skin. I know it's awful, Bobby, but I really wish that we could just put our arms around each other and roll down a beautiful hill for ever. We'd just roll and roll and you could tell me all sorts of headlines and talk about the goodness that should exist, and tell me about your utopia. Your dream will come. If you think my hair is too straight, I'll get it cut and curl it for you. And then something struck her and made her stand frozen, almost afraid to turn around. The white rabbit coat had been bothering her for some reason, and the smell of gardenias, too, for that matter. She knew that the coat was only worth about $160. She knew that she herself had turned one down because she had wanted a clock-radio instead. But what was really wrong about that white rabbit coat was that it was too chintzy for Mrs Hulka. Mrs Hulka wouldn't own such a coat. Mrs Hulka was at times gaudy but not a thing she wore was·cheap. And the smell of gardenias that had been in the room, that bothered her, too. Lauri had noticed the moment she met Mrs Hulka that she was into Chanel and she had seen the Chanel bottle on her vanity. Mrs Hulka was Chanel and mink, not gardenias and rabbit fur, and, what was worse, she suddenly realized that the coat on that dummy looked much too short for Mrs Hulka. Of course, maybe Mrs Hulka had saved it from when she was a kid and wore it to a teenage prom and was just getting ready to donate it to the Volunteers of America as a tax write-off.

Lauri suddenly defrosted, turned around and began to walk swiftly back. It was really dark by the time she reached the dent in the hedges where she had left Bobby.

'Bobby,' she called softly. She called his name a dozen times, but there was no answer. Some branches scraped her face as she turned to look at the funeral home. 'Baby Jesus,' she prayed, crossing herself. She took a deep breath and decided that the best attack would be a direct one. She marched straight down the driveway towards Mr

Hulka's station-wagon. She kept calling 'Bobby' in a hoarse whisper, addressing the hedges, hoping he was still hiding somewhere behind them, and maybe would pop out so they could just clear out. She was aware of how strange she must look, hesitating and talking to hedges. If anyone was watching her approach the house, they had every right to mistake her for a crazy person and shoot her or let Doberman pinschers come out and attack her. Well, enough of those thoughts, she decided, as she reached Mr Hulka's station-wagon. 'Bobby, Bobby,' she began to call in a louder voice, but still there was no response. She walked briskly to the lighted door of the annexe and gave a firm knock. There were only three choices as far as she was concerned. First, that Bobby was inside, about to get into trouble. Or second, that he was already in trouble, and Mr Hulka was calling the police to report him. And the third was that she herself would be able to head the trouble off by explaining the impetuousness of youth to Mr Hulka. Certainly even undertakers were kids once. As her hand connected with the door, she was surprised to see the door swing open from the force of her knock, and her eyes widened into lollipops as she saw she was in a casket supermarket. There was no way her eyes could fly to anything except the exquisite silver coffin on the highest tier, and when she saw a body bolt upright in the coffin's interior, she reached her hands to her throat to let out a scream. The pocket of air that ran up her breathing tube and would have formed the scream was almost out of her mouth before she recognized it was Bobby sitting in the coffin and making incredibly dramatic gestures.

'What are you doing?' Lauri asked.

'Beat it,' Bobby said in a tiny frantic voice.

'I will not beat it,' Lauri said, walking right up the steps of the platforms. 'We're both getting out of here before we *do* end up in a reform school for wayward ghouls.' Lauri's body suffered a minor spasm when she heard a door slam somewhere from another part of the building.

It was the sound of metal clanging and it wasn't a dragging chain, but pretty close to it. Lauri reached into the coffin and tried to pull Bobby out, but instead he grabbed her and pulled her right into the coffin.

'He's coming,' Bobby wheezed. Lauri was in the uncomfortable position of having her rear end in the coffin and her legs dangling out. There was something about Bobby's latest information that made her legs zip quick like a bunny in and under the closed portion of the coffin, as though she had rather impetuously accepted an invitation to share a sleeping-bag. Her face was smack next to Bobby's and a part of her wanted to really yell and get the whole thing over with, just get caught and get out and explain that it was all just a sort of faux pas that the two of them had ended up in a coffin together; fall upon the mercy of whoever was coming, to just forgive and forget and not call the police for trespassing. She began to open her mouth but then found Bobby's hand had wriggled its way up from between their bodies and smacked itself against her mouth. They were eyeball to eyeball as the sound of the clanging metal got louder; heavy, heavy objects swinging, hitting against each other. Lauri tried to turn her head slightly to make sure her nostrils could get enough oxygen, but all she could see was the sides of the coffin and above her the ceiling with the light that made her think she was about to undergo an autopsy. It was all like being trapped in some grotesque crib. Trapped was the right word, she decided, because she could hear all the sounds very clearly now. Her ears told her there was somebody moving around the room.

She stopped fighting Bobby. She even relaxed enough to wiggle her hand up from between their bodies to pull his left thumb away from her nose because it was tickling her. Now there were three hands resting on her chin, one was her own and both of Bobby's, which she had yanked downward to free all her air passages. Bobby was trying rather vainly to tell some sort of story with his eyes, but she 'hadn't the faintest idea what it was. He moved one finger to his lips to re-create the universally accepted sign for her to shut up. In fact, he made the gesture so many times she felt like telling him she wasn't retarded. She simply could not believe she was in a casket. *Bobby Perkins really knows how to show a girl a good time.*

Finally the metal clinking stopped and Lauri heard the footsteps retreat. A shadow fell across the ceiling indicating whoever it was was going back to the main house.

'Hulka's making a pile of metal hands,' Bobby said.

'I beg your pardon?' Lauri enquired.

'He's making a pile of metal hands behind the platforms.'

She hadn't the faintest idea what he was talking about. 'Let's get out of here,' she said. 'He's coming back.' Lauri even raised the front of her body in protest. Her head swung upward in an arc and she tried to get a grip on the side of the casket. It was all a bit like being a discontented sardine in a can. Bobby kept pulling her downward and she was trying to pop out, but then she caught a glimpse of the strange metal objects on the floor not far from the casket. Bobby hadn't been kidding. There were dozens of little metal rods. The rods had tiny metal hands that opened like clothes-pins attached at regular intervals. Three-foot rods with nine or ten little hands protruding, rods which had heavy iron bases attached to them. Again came the clinking of metal and Lauri slipped back to her burial position.

· 'What *are* they?' Lauri whispered.

'They use them to hold money cards,' Bobby said, 'when people come to Italian funerals and things like that. Instead of sending flowers, they give cards to the family and then the cards get stuck in the little hands and they're on display along with the flowers.'

'Oh, my God,' Lauri said. She had only been to a couple of funerals but hadn't noticed those things around. The only time she saw anything that looked like it, it was a special rod to hold guest towels in a bathroom.

The shadow of a man moved across the ceiling again, its shape distorted, multiplied by the many light sources. Now the metallic sounds seemed more orderly. Whatever was being done with the metal hands and the rods and the heavy bases was being done with more urgency. Then came the sounds of the metal bases, thuds, moving away towards the exit of the annexe, towards the night outside. Bobby clapped one hand over Lauri's mouth and this time he leaned up, lifting his face to a point where the light from the room could crash into his eyes. Lauri watched his pupils grow small but anxious. Then the lights were switched off and there was the sound of the casket show-room door being closed. But she had left it open. If it was Mr Hulka, wouldn't he have noticed it? Although maybe it closed by itself. Maybe it was arranged to swing on a pneumatic contraption that would seal it silently. The worst thing would be that he knew they were in there. Even if he was waiting, the worst thing, she thought, that would happen was he would have them arrested for tres-passing and make them pay for wearing dirty shoes in that classy coffin.

'He's opening the back panel of the station-wagon,' Bobby reported.

'What else?'

'He's opening a suitcase.'

'Can you see what's in it?'

'No, it's too deep. I can just see part of it through the window. He's sticking the rods with the metal hands into it. I think I see a foot.'

'A foot?'

'Yes,' Bobby said. 'I think he just lifted a foot and stuck a metal base under it. He's packing the suitcase with metal.'

Lauri was listening for all she was worth. She heard the sound of the station-wagon door slamming. It seemed like he had slammed the rear panel very hard and then had opened probably the driver's door, slammed that, but it hadn't closed. and then there was a louder slam that probably did the job, she decided. She didn't need Bobby to tell her that the motor had just been started. She knew the moment the headlights went on because eruptions of light sprung through the windows, creating shadows of dancing coffins.

'He's making a U-turn in the driveway,' Bobby informed her.

'Phew,' Lauri sighed, feeling much safer. She was certain now they hadn't been seen. They could get out of there. She even relaxed enough to realize that she was truly, truly lying in a casket, and how proper that was, in a sense, she thought, because didn't they put Sleeping Beauty in a casket? No, she remembered, that was Snow White. Maybe in some versions of Sleeping Beauty she ended up in a casket, too. Maybe that was it. It was hard to tell really where Snow White and Sleeping Beauty left off. Besides, she thought she probably was a mixture of both of them. And besides, both of those girls had occupied their caskets alone. The prince hadn't been rammed into the thing with her, and certainly not under such un-glamorous circumstances as these. Wouldn't it be incred-ible, she thought, if Bobby just suddenly looked down at her, rotated slightly on a horizontal axis, and kissed her, saying, 'I love you, Lauri. I love you passionately.' And she would say, 'Oh, Bobby, I knew you would come and bring me to life.' And he would kiss her, and they would get up out of the casket and climb on a white stallion with a golden bridle and they would ride up Main Street, out of Leonia, and into Fort Lee, and live happily ever after; but she knew the timing would be a little off, under the circumstances.

'Come on,' Bobby blurted, jumping up and out of the casket. He practically tossed Lauri out and into a vertical position. He grabbed her hand and dragged her with giant steps down the platforms to the floor level. The lights of the station-wagon were just curving to the right at the end of the driveway. Bobby seemed to be galloping with only one idea in his head.

'You're ripping my arm out of its socket,' Lauri complained, as they bounded out of the annexe door. The garage loomed like a mausoleum, as Bobby kept her running through the night air. 'You're going the wrong way,' she complained, as he half slid her around the back of the house. '*The chauffeur!*' she frantically reminded him as they began to cross the mid-section of the backyard. The columns of the breezeway, with the hearse snuggled beneath it, began to come into view.

'Pinocchio's probably watching TV or pickling something in the cellar,' Bobby spurted more hopefully than factually. He came to a sudden halt on the driver's side of the hearse, swung open the door, jumped in, and grabbed for the steering column. He was delighted to find the keys greeting his twitching fingers. 'Get in,' he ordered Lauri, pulling her right across his lap and landing her into what is colloquially called the suicide seat.

'Bobby, I've heard of auto theft,' Lauri stated, 'but this is ridiculous.'

'He's got her body in that suitcase,' Bobby yelled, starting the hearse. Without putting on the lights, he wheeled it quickly around the back of the house and in a flash was hurtling down the driveway.

'He's got metal hands that hold money cards in that suitcase.'

'And a body,' Bobby insisted. He checked left for traffic and then threw on his headlights, swinging wide out on to the main street. It took Lauri a full minute to get enough oxygen into her haemoglobin and to right herself properly. Now she was furious. 'This time you *have* gone too far.' And she yelled it hysterically, six times, until she happened to turn around and look at the long empty space and curtained windows which comprised the rear of the hearse. It was like a great gaping chasm chasing them. That shut her up and she spun back and sat, frozen, staring at the front windshield, both hands on the dashboard as they started the ascent into Fort Lee.

'He's heading for the river,' Bobby said, straining to see ahead. Several pairs of taillights were flickering in the distance, but Lauri's eyes weren't good enough to define exactly which ones belonged to Hulka's station-wagon.

'Bobby, you don't know how to drive a hearse,' she reminded him.

'It's just like my father's station-wagon.'

'Oh, baby Jesus, there's the police.' Lauri pointed wildly.

'Where?'

'There.' She pinpointed the next intersection.

'They're stopped at a red light,' Bobby observed.

'But won't they get suspicious if they see a speeding hearse?'

Bobby decided to detour from Main Street. He made a sharp left and then a right and landed on one of the approach roadways for the George Washington Bridge. At the last opportunity he swung sharply to the right to catch the final exit before the bridge, and then snaked the hearse through a series of side streets heading for River Road. At one point they sped by a cop car that was heading in the opposite direction.

'Uh-oh. I think they noticed us,' Lauri said.

Bobby braked and then made a turn into one of the side roads which would take them right to the river's edge. He put the lights out just in case the cops had doubled back, and hardly noticed any change in the illumination because of the massive string of lights from the bridge which stretched out high to the left above them, lights thrusting to the New York side of the Hudson. At last the road ended and gave way to the sheet of dancing wavelets. Bobby brought the hearse to a stop, leaped out and started running out on to the point of land which jutted several hundred feet into the river. He picked this point because he knew it was the one spot he would be able to see a good distance in either direction along the bank. To the left was only darkness; to the right were the docks. One was for fishing, another was for small boats, and a third was old and deserted except for a recognizable long, black station-wagon. Its headlights were on and Bobby could see a figure limping, bent by a burden. Lauri caught up to Bobby and they both stood and watched the distant tableau of a man far away moving out on to a pier and throwing a large rectangular object into the river.

Chapter 12

Lauri refused to talk to Bobby as they got back into the hearse and he drove to Main Street. So what if Mr Hulka had thrown a suitcase into the river? she told herself. It's probably just some old garbage, including the strange little metal hands. And maybe he *was* just throwing something out. Mr Hulka certainly wouldn't be the first person to pollute the Hudson River. All anyone had to do was take a train ride along the New York side and they'd see all sorts of things thrown down the edge of the hills, refrigerators, mattresses, old sinks and toilets, all sorts of bags of non-biodegradable garbage, suitcases included.

'Where are we going now?' Lauri asked.

'Here,' Bobby said, turning the wheel and pulling the hearse into the McDonald's hamburger parking lot.

'Are you out of your mind!' Lauri screeched, noticing that the entire group of kids sitting at the outdoor tables paused in mid-bites to gape at the gigantic grey vehicle slithering into a parking place.

'Somebody's got to believe us,' Bobby emphasized.

'*I* don't believe us,' Lauri protested. 'Bobby, the police are going to get us.'

'Good,' Bobby interrupted. 'Somebody's got to take an interest. Let's get the kids on our side. That's the best chance we've got.'

'Aren't you being melodramatic?'

'What's that?'

'I don't know,' Lauri admitted.

Everyone was still staring as Bobby got out of the hearse. He walked around to Lauri's side and opened the door for her as though they had just arrived at the Copacabana.

'My legs are shaking,' Lauri admitted.

'Don't worry. I'll take care of everything,' Bobby assured her. 'The kids will believe us. I know it.'

Lauri reached out and held on to the fancy long chrome handles which lined the rear section of the hearse. It was all very shiny and vinyl covered, like an elegant stretched baby-carriage. She tried to straighten up so she wouldn't leave too many fingerprints, but then she got a really good look at all the faces inside McDonald's. The whole interior of the emporium looked like a giant goldfish bowl with feeding time coming up.

'I can't do it,' Lauri said.

'All right,' he said. 'You stay in the hearse, and I'll get help.'

'No,' Lauri said, shivering. 'I'll just sit here on the rear bumper.'

'You sure?'

'I'm really sure,' Lauri said, feeling as though she was front and centre on a huge stage.

Bobby gave her a quick squeeze on the left shoulder. 'I'll be right back,' he said with determination, turned and jogged right over to the first outdoor table, the one where all the big wheels from Fort Lee High were sitting. She watched him break right into the group, who were still absolutely mesmerized by the sight of the hearse, and the only thing that comforted her was moving her hand to where Bobby had touched her. Uh-oh, she thought, he's telling David Banani, and Lucille Cutlet, and Vinnie Fink, and Hank Thompson, and Gigi Whatever-her-name-is. Well, that is crazy, she thought. You don't just jump out of a hearse at McDonald's and run up to a table of kids, especially the crème de la crème of Fort Lee High, and tell them that the undertaker who lives next door to you has just thrown his wife in the Hudson River with a bunch of metal hands. I mean, that is a little much. *You don't do that*, she wanted to yell out. *They'll think you're crazy, Bobby. They'll make fun of you and hurt you, just like they always do in school. You know what they're like. They only care about controlling who gets on the varsity* teams and the cheer-leading squads and into the GO government. She could see that several of the kids were already laughing at him, muffling, hiding their grins. They were listening and already they were laughing, giving smart glances to each other, particularly that stuck-up David Banani and Lucille Cutlet who were always kissing in their car right in front of the school every day, the big football hero and the junior class treasurer, both of them the nastiest couple in the world. *Don't tell them any more, Bobby*, she wanted to call out. *They don't like people.* Baby Jesus, she prayed to herself, don't let them hurt his feelings. Don't let them call him a jerk and idiot, like they usually do. I don't care what they think of me but, please God, don't let them hurt Bobby.

But now they were laughing right in his face and calling to other tables. She could see Bobby was talking a mile a minute, trying desperately to get them to help, to believe him. Now there were donkey-sized laughs, including a horrid senior named Ann Sommers, who thought she was God's gift to the parallel bars. Annie Sommers was the same one who had made fun of Lauri in an English class once when Lauri had to stand up and give a speech on the most frightening thing that had ever happened to her, when she told the class about that night in Edison. Lauri had dug out a quote from someone that said, 'Death is not a foe but an inevitable adventure', and right off the bat Annie Sommers had let out this phony shriek of laughter and made Lauri feel so terrible she couldn't go on with her speech. An inevitable adventure, Lauri remembered, her back straightening and touching the rear door of the hearse. It made her think just then about how many caskets had slid in and out of right where she was sitting. How many more would be popped in and popped out, people that had once been alive, with important feelings? Some of them had to be people who maybe lived their whole lives and had never found any fulfilment because they were snuffed out and kicked around by kids with dispositions like Annie Sommers and Davie Banani and Lucille Cutlet. Now it seemed the entire spread of kids at the tables were gnashing at their french fries and sesame-seed buns, mocking uproariously, pointing and searing Bobby with their disbelief as though he were the Hunchback of Notre Dame. Before she knew what happened she was on her feet and yelling at the top of her lungs, yelling at all those little snots who had nothing better to do than to squat on their little behinds at some hamburger joint all night and gossip and destroy other kids' reputations and not reach out a hand to help some guy who didn't happen to quite fit into their mould at that moment. 'Don't you laugh at him!' Lauri screamed. 'Don't you laugh.' And for a moment they all shut up and again she was the centre of attention. Even the people inside had heard her, kids squashing their faces against the windows again. Bobby looked so sad, because he realized it really was a hopeless situation. He came directly to Lauri and helped her back into the hearse. The kids were jeering viciously at them now, making cow sounds and literally lying on the benches weak from their mob hysteria.

Bobby got into the driver's seat. Lauri watched him and felt very deeply for his hurt, for the things they must have said to him that she hadn't heard.

'Hold on,' Bobby commanded, throwing the hearse into reverse. He shot the vehicle backward and stopped on a dime and threw the shift into drive and squealed behind the building, only to pop out again on the other side and barrel past the standing, booing ovation the kids were now giving. He had to come to a quick halt at the exit sign to wait for a break in the traffic. Finally it came and he propelled the hearse out on to Main Street. He drove out of sight of McDonald's and then pulled the hearse to a stop at the side of the road.

'We're ditching this here,' he explained.

Lauri automatically leaned over with a tissue and quickly wiped the steering wheel to get rid of fingerprints.

'Don't bother,' Bobby said as Lauri got out and ran to

wipe the door handles. 'Hurry up,' he said, already beginning to walk quickly towards the huge tower of lights a
block away, the tower known as the Century Tower
Apartments. 'We've got a killer to catch,' Bobby blurted
over his shoulder, slapping his thigh like a concerned
master summoning a puppy who had finally earned the
right to join fully a great hunt.

An inevitable adventure, Lauri thought, as she ran to
catch up.

Chapter 13

Joe the Schmo was still on duty and spotted Lauri and Bobby the moment they made their approach to the canopy. He screamed at them like an insane man as they went through the revolving door. Bobby put his arm around Lauri and just walked slowly, letting Joe the Schmo leap from side to side in his silly baggy uniform, making all sorts of threats, but Bobby knew that Joe wouldn't dare lay a hand on them.

'You stained the marble,' Joe kept repeating. 'It took an hour to get the garbage up. The cans and the carrots and the broken glass.'

'He's killed his wife,' Bobby said calmly, all the time moving towards the elevators.

'I don't have to pick up after kids,' Joe kept on. 'And the porters don't either. We're not hired for that.'

Bobby spoke with great control. 'Joe, I'm telling you that Mr Hulka has killed his wife, dumped her in the river, and you're talking to me about a little garbage.'

'You're crazy.'

'Maybe you're right,' Bobby said.

'You kids think you can do anything,' Joe brayed.

'No, we don't,' Bobby said, holding the door for Lauri to enter one of the elevators.

Joe the Schmo looked ready to explode. 'When your father and mother get back I'm telling them everything you did and your father's going to beat you to a pulp.'

Bobby looked him right in the eye. 'You'll be lucky if he doesn't beat you up,' Bobby said. 'In fact, you'll be lucky if I don't have you arrested for loitering in this lobby.' Bobby pressed the button marked 24 and the doors started closing.

'I told your mother,' Joe the Schmo said, pointing his

finger at Lauri. 'I told your mother you're hanging around with a young bum. That's what I told her, and she's going to . . .'

The elevator lifted them out of range of Joe's voice. Joe's last remark struck Lauri's heart like an arrow. Now she was not only worried about Bobby being arrested for trespassing, hearse stealing, garbage splattering and tenant libelling, she felt the distinct pain that her own mother and father must be very worried.

'Maybe we should go straight to my apartment,' she suggested.

'No,' Bobby said. 'They won't let you out again.'

Lauri felt a flush of joy in the sense that she was really needed by Bobby, and she thought that for one time it was more important to stick with Bobby and at least make one more attempt to let him know he was acting rather irrational and needed to get things in perspective. It was as though the entire event had become like the Unicorn tapestry at The Cloisters. There were too many threads, too many colours, forms, visions, woven into aspects not easy to understand.

Bobby put his arm around Lauri as they hurtled upward in the machine. He looked down at her as though he was having second thoughts.

'I don't want to make you go back to my apartment if you're really afraid.'

'I'm not,' Lauri said.

'Hulka could be waiting for us,' Bobby admitted. 'Maybe it would be better if you did just go to your place.'

Lauri put her arm around his waist and they stood very close. 'I want to talk to you about that,' she said.

'Even though he's got rid of the body, he still may feel he has to kill us.'

The elevator door opened and Lauri preceded Bobby out and down the hall. Bobby had to skip to catch up to her, and he could tell something had set off a rush of adrenalin in her. She seemed more disturbed than afraid. He fumbled in his pockets, found his keys and unlocked the door. Lauri walked right in, started turning on all the lights she could get her hands on, and sat down on the living-room sofa between two piles of junk from Mrs Perkins's art endeavours. She folded her hands, crossed her legs and watched impatiently while Bobby rammed a chair under the front doorknob and then darted to the terrace door to make sure its lock was in place.

'What's the matter?' Bobby asked, noticing that there was obviously something wrong with her.

'Well, you are making me very uptight,' Lauri said, still managing to keep a lid on the column of air in her lungs that was about ready to erupt.

'Well,' Bobby said, 'I've got one thing to say to you, and that is that I'm very proud of you.'

That did it.

'Proud of me?' Lauri asked exasperatedly. 'For what? For letting you do all this?'

'All what?'

'Bobby, the jig's up,' Lauri underlined. 'I've got to call my mother and tell her everything she's heard about the police and the garbage and everything else is true.'

'You're right,' Bobby agreed. 'As long as she calls the police. They'll believe her. Better yet, have your father call.'

'I'll do no such thing,' Lauri stated. 'Bobby, you've got to stop this.'

'A lady's been murdered and you say I've got to stop this?'

'Nobody's been murdered.'

'You heard her screaming.'

'I heard a fight.'

'But I *saw* it.'

'*You* saw a dummy in a blonde wig and a cheap rabbit coat,' Lauri said, trying to stick to the facts, now that she wasn't alone walking home through the dark. After everything that had gone down, her Chanel No. 5 and gardenias and rabbit-fur theory was nothing but circumstantial evidence she now wanted to believe. Bobby's suspicions were simply intermittently contagious.

'Maybe that was a mistake.'

'Bobby, if you've been inventing all this for me, I beg you, please, please stop it.'

'I didn't invent it for you.'

'If you wanted me not to be afraid of dying, fire, or anything else, let me clue you in. You succeeded,' she said sincerely.

'I have?' Bobby asked, as though it came as a complete surprise to him that she thought he had been using psychology on her all along.

Lauri got up and began to pace around the room, knocking into some of Mr Perkins's inventions. The small butane torch rolled off Mrs Perkins's metal sculpture corner. Lauri picked the torch up and slapped it back down on the table. 'Yes, you have at last made me completely unafraid of dying. You've got me into positions I've never dreamed of, not the least of which has been a catnap in a crowded coffin,' Lauri reminded him.

Bobby stared at her disbelievingly. 'Lauri, lots of times I was trying to help you, but not today. Today is real.'

'Oh, no, it's not,' Lauri insisted.

'Mrs Hulka is dead. She's at the bottom of the Hudson River,' Bobby said factually.

'Now stop it,' Lauri insisted, running for the terrace door. 'If you still think I'm afraid of heights, forget it, I'm not.'

'Don't,' Bobby cried out.

Before Bobby could stop her she had unlocked the door and walked out on the terrace. He dashed out after her and saw her leaning over the railing, breathing deeply of the night air. Lauri explained, 'I'm not afraid of anything crazy any more, of midgets falling on my head, of irresponsible people locking me in a washing machine, or of finding poisonous worms in my alphabet soup. If that's what you wanted to drive me to, you've done it. You've got me so exasperated and terrified, that by now there's not an ounce of fright left in me for anything except your sanity. The only thing I'm worried about is you,' Lauri said, her voice becoming suddenly gentle.

Bobby stood against the railing next to her. The echo of her words was still bouncing off the cliff rocks and firing themselves back at the terrace.

'Gee, that's swell,' Bobby said, squeezing her right shoulder.

'And would you stop squeezing my shoulders,' Lauri requested, not really meaning it. What she wanted to say was, *Why don't you take me in your arms and kiss me and make believe we're just a plain old normal boy and girl who could fall in love with each other if we gave each other half a chance?*

'Please, Bobby,' she said. 'Just not being afraid of dying isn't enough to make life worthwhile. I think I'm ready for the next step.'

She could tell by the look in his eyes that romance was still not quite in the air. She had seen that look before in someone else's eyes, and she realized it was in her own eyes when she used to stare at herself in the mirror. It was the look of an alarmed person. She took another deep breath and this time just rocked forward, looking at the exquisitely lit bridge. Then she realized her right shoulder was touching the partition which separated them from Hulka's balcony. She turned her head and let her glance crawl along the cement of that balcony and then accelerated it through the glass doors into the Hulka living-room.

Bobby reached out to take her hand. 'Move away from the partition,' he said slowly, his voice crackling with concern.

'Why?' Lauri asked, without turning her head to look at him.

'He could grab you,' Bobby said.

Lauri burst into laughter, and then looked directly at Bobby. Bobby looked at her, shocked. He was dumbfounded. He had done such a good job on her. That was nice, but it seemed like something had struck her as inordinately funny. He pulled her away from the divider, but she was still laughing so hard she actually fell against the glass door; the tough Thermopane hardly budged.

'What's so funny?' Bobby wanted to know.

Lauri couldn't stop howling enough to speak a word, so she simply pointed to the partition. Bobby bounded to the railing's edge and looked around to see whatever it was that sent her into such a fit of giggles. He froze at the sight, as though he were a kid staring at a magic show in which the most extraordinary trick had just been performed.

'Wow,' he said.

There in the Hulkas' living-room was Mrs Hulka, reading a book. She was sitting in a straight-back wooden chair and he could see only the back of her head, the coiffure perfect and rising above the same golden-flowered feather-trimmed robe she had worn when they had first invaded with the Welcome Wagon. This certainly wasn't a dummy, because there was one real arm and a very real hand holding a martini glass. Her other hand was holding an open book, a large book resting against a crossed leg. Bobby moved to the slit between the partition and the brick wall to see if he could make out enough profile to be absolutely certain that it really was Mrs Hulka. He could see her left eyelid and part of her left nostril and that was about it. If she would just set the drink down on the cheap elephant table, he would probably be able to get a good look at her face.

Lauri managed to make it into the living-room and Bobby came shuffling in after her.

'I was sure he had killed her,' Bobby sighed.

Lauri had one more series of giggles to get out, and then she finally composed herself. This time she put her arm around Bobby and pulled him on to the sofa with her. 'You sound sorry he didn't,' she said half scoldingly.

Bobby kept turning his head, looking over his shoulder towards the terrace. Lauri thought he looked so cute when he was discombobulated, so this time she squeezed *his* shoulder and then went directly to the house phone.

'Who are you calling?' Bobby asked.

'I've got to call my mother,' Lauri said.

'Then we've got to figure out what to do about reporting the hearse, at least make an anonymous call and tell them where it is.'

'Hello,' Lauri heard her mother's voice come on the phone.

'Hi, Mom,' Lauri said.

'Lauri, where are you?' Mrs Geddes asked with concern.

'I'm up at Bobby's and everything's just fine,' Lauri started, but then her mother called forth a rush of everything she'd heard. Lauri just kept watching Bobby sitting slightly stunned, his head still turning towards the window. Mrs Geddes covered all the reports of their soiling the foyer and jumping into taxis, and that the police had been there, and that Bobby had invented some story about a murder.

'I'm sorry, but most of it's true,' Lauri said, 'but it's all over now.'

'Oh, I'm so glad,' her mother said.

'Everything's fine. I'm fine. Bobby's fine,' Lauri said convincingly. 'We're up in his apartment. We're going to have a little tea and have a good laugh about the whole thing.'

'Well,' her mother said. 'You know, your father and I were a little worried, but we know Joe the Schmo is a shnook.'

Lauri laughed and wished she was right next to her mother then so she could give her a big squeeze. She could hear her father asking questions in the background and she waited while her mother relayed the information.

'And Bobby's all right?' her mother wanted to know.

Lauri watched as Bobby rushed back out on to the terrace to peer around the partition.

'Fine,' Lauri said.

'Well, bring him down for dinner,' her mother insisted.

'What are we having?'

'Pork loin.'

Lauri knew that was one of Bobby's favourites. 'Okay,' she said, 'but I think he needs to calm down a bit first. He's out on the terrace getting some fresh air.'

'He can get fresh air down here,' her mother said.

'Mom, he's fine, but he's just quieting down a little bit. We have a few things to talk over. We'll be down in about an hour or so. Okay?'

'All right, honey,' her mother said. 'You know, it sounds as though you're taking care of him for a change.'

Lauri looked up to see that Bobby had come back into the living-room and was pacing like a young lion in front of her, waiting for her to hang up.

'I think you're right,' Lauri said. 'See you in a little while, okay?'

'Okay,' her mother signed off merrily. Lauri let out a big sigh. She was just about to ask Bobby if he would like some tea or cocoa when there came a distinct clicking sound, a metallic swooping sound that lasted only a few seconds. In a flash Bobby was out at the railing peering around the partition again. Lauri walked nonchalantly to the doorway. 'Would you like tea or cocoa?' Lauri asked sweetly.

'The drapes are closed,' Bobby said.

'That's nice,' Lauri commented, and then proceeded with what she thought was the more important issue. 'I asked whether you would like tea or cocoa.'

'Why would they close the drapes?' Bobby asked.

'Why not?' Lauri posed.

'Because they never close the drapes,' Bobby informed her. 'Not more than that once since they moved in here have they ever closed the drapes, and I've been snooping on them almost every night.'

'I think they know that now,' Lauri said, 'so I think you can expect to see the drapes closed a whole lot in the future. My mother's made pork loin,' Lauri added, changing the tack. 'And you know how much you like pork loin. I told her we'd be down in a little while.'

'Come over here,' Bobby said without turning to look

at her. Lauri groaned and swung her head below Bobby's so now they were both staring around the partition. The drapes were open again now and Mr Hulka was standing with his back to the window, talking to Mrs Hulka. Lauri couldn't understand what he was saying but it seemed to be something about getting some fresh ice or making a new drink. He was wearing a lounge robe, but Lauri could see he still had slacks and shoes on, which did seem a bit incongruous. She always thought the rich just plopped around in expensive leather slippers and silk pyjamas under their smoking jackets. They could still see Mr Hulka talking as he approached his wife, who was now in the hammock. She was in the Guatemalan hammock with all the colours, and now it looked as though she was watching television, but still balancing her drink on her stomach.

'Why did they open and close the drapes?' Bobby whispered.

'They changed their mind. Maybe it got too dark to watch TV or whatever,' Lauri offered.

What bothered Bobby the most was that it was still impossible to see Mrs Hulka's face. They could see her feet spread upward on the far curve of the hammock in the corner. They could see one hand entwined in the strings of her hair at the other end as though she was extremely comfortable, and you could see the other hand holding the drink. Then Mr Hulka turned and they could see that he was chatting with her some more, laughing; he even went to tickle his wife. It all looked a bit like a very warm exchange but what was a little disturbing was that the only voice they could hear was Mr Hulka's. Mr Hulka went to a sideboard and mixed a new drink and then he sort of did a little dance or was obviously telling a very funny joke to Mrs Hulka. He seemed so debonair that even his eyes lost their generally evil cast, and the lines in his face seemed softer in what was rather dim light. Through all this, Mrs Hulka didn't move and she didn't take a drink and then finally Mr Hulka came back to the edge of the window and Lauri yanked her head away but Bobby refused to compromise his vantage point. They could both hear Mr Hulka laughing and in the middle of some comment about how amusing something was on television, he mentioned the name Veronica three or four times and then pulled the drapes closed again.

'It's like a show,' Bobby whispered, coming back from the railing and looking at Lauri. 'He's opening and closing those curtains like there's some kind of play going on.'

Lauri didn't say anything. She just went back inside and put some water on to boil.

Bobby joined her in the kitchen, watching her set up the cups and getting the tea bags out of a porcelain jar shaped like a wild boar.

'There's something wrong,' Bobby said.

Lauri didn't say anything. She just kept fussing and refussing with the tea preparations, straightening the teacups, checking the flame beneath the kettle. The fact that she didn't respond immediately told Bobby that now maybe she too felt something was not quite right. Suddenly the idea struck Bobby to do something rather daring. He picked up the house phone. The only two numbers he had memorized were 101, which was the concierge, and 118, which was the garage. So he had to rummage through one of the kitchen drawers which contained all the appliance guarantees and other booklets until he found the in-house telephone book. The in-house telephone number for 24G was 6283, and Bobby dialled it. He could hear it ringing several times. Finally a man answered and Bobby recognized Mr Hulka's voice.

'May I please speak to *Mrs* Hulka?' Bobby enquired.

There was a long pause. Finally the voice on the other end said, 'Who's calling, please?'

'A friend,' Bobby said calculatedly. 'A very good friend.'

'I'm sorry, but Mrs Hulka's retired for the evening,' the voice said. 'Is there a message I can give her?'

Lauri moved closer to Bobby, inching her ear to the receiver so she could overhear. Bobby weighed the clever tone he sensed in Mr Hulka's last remark and decided to take the plunge.

'Yes,' Bobby said firmly. 'Tell her I think she's dead.'

There was a very long pause this time and Lauri was getting that 'Oh-Bobby-you've-really-gone-over-the-hill-this-time' look on her face, but her ear snuggled in closer and closer to the receiver until now she was earlobe to earlobe with Bobby.

'Is there anything else?' Mr Hulka's voice enquired.

Bobby realized his hand was beginning to vibrate slightly. He was embarrassed that the receiver was practically bouncing between his and Lauri's heads. He gripped the bottom of their receiver with his other hand to steady it, and he knew he could only utter at best one more coherent sentence.

'You'll never get her body out,' Bobby said loudly and clearly, 'because we'll be watching.'

Then there came the sound of a disconnect. Bobby slowly hung up the phone. Lauri silently returned to the stove to check on the water. She wanted to say something about how they should call the police to tell them where the hearse was, just that anonymous call. Mr Hulka would know *his* phone call was a joke, she was positive. And she wanted to say something about the pork loin again and they could just go down and have a nice, safe dinner and how they should just get out of that apartment even though it was all in their imagination. She felt so stupid when the only thing that came out of her mouth was a cliché. 'A watched pot never boils,' Lauri mumbled.

'We'll see about that,' Bobby said, regaining a grip on matters. He moved quickly to the terrace door to lock it, and then he checked the front door to make certain it was locked and the chair was firmly in place, wedged under the doorknob. On close inspection, he didn't really think the chair would help because it just wasn't long enough and if someone really wanted to break in, it would probably begin to slide. Lauri came into the living-room carrying their teacups on a platter and she was beginning to look scared again, so Bobby just tossed the chair to the side as though they really didn't need any protection. No one would be breaking down the door.

Lauri placed the brew on a small square shiny table which Mrs Perkins had constructed during her zinc period. Besides, it was the only spot in the entire living-room which had two chairs more conducive to conversation than to supporting creative paraphernalia.

'Careful, it's a bit hot,' Lauri said as Bobby joined her. Bobby could tell Lauri was really frightened now because it was the first time he had ever noticed her skin become the absolute colour of an albino's. He didn't quite know what to say to make things better. He thought of saying, 'Hey, honey, there's nothing to be worried about,' but he knew she would be able to tell just from his voice that he was more than just concerned about matters himself. She might even sense a speck of fear in him. Maybe he should just admit it to her and they could go down and have the pork roast and he could sleep over on the couch downstairs and everything would seem different in the morning. There was something about the nighttime that always made things seem more sinister than they really were. He always remembered that the worst time for human beings was four o'clock in the morning because that was when most people die and which a lot of poets call the Hour of the Wolf.

'If you're sure he's killed her, let's just hurry on down and tell my mother and father,' Lauri said. 'We can tell them right in person.'

'No,' Bobby said.

'Why not?'

Bobby took a sip of tea, pretending to relax in a chair. 'Well, I suppose because if we went out the door, Mr Hulka might be glued to the peephole this time and really come hacking at us with the cleaver, if you want to know the truth.'

Lauri felt a few more corpuscles fleeing from her cheeks as she added a teaspoon of sugar to her cup. 'Well, then,

I'll call them on the phone and have them come up and get us,' she suggested. 'Unless, of course, you think Hulka will pop out and hack all of us to death, in which case I'll have my mother call the police.'

Bobby thought that one over a minute. 'No good.'

'Why?'

'Can you just see what your mother and father would do if you told them to call the police because you thought our lives were in danger and they shouldn't come up because we might all be hacked to death?'

'They'd both come running to get us,' Lauri said.

'You know what I think?' Bobby asked.

'What?'

'I really think this whole thing is a tempest in a teapot.' Bobby looked at her very seriously and then burst into laughter. Lauri looked at him over the rim of her cup and the joke got to her. She exploded into laughter, too, practically spraying the table with a mouthful of tea. They laughed louder and louder and finally the two of them were on the floor. Bobby was rolling and rocking and Lauri crawled after him, telling him to stop or she was going to absolutely die laughing. The release they needed had finally come.

'You're going to *die* laughing?' Bobby managed to enquire, and then fell into a fit of renewed laughter. He laughed so hard he couldn't speak. They hadn't laughed so much since they had got dressed up as a monk and a nun, or maybe it was the time they had worn the masks on the bridge. And then there was the time that they had even gone roller skating through a pack of commuters at the Henry Hudson Bus Terminal. They collided and Lauri was in Bobby's arms as they rolled back and forth on the floor, laughing hysterically. They laughed so long and so hard that by the time they stopped neither could move or talk.

'My sides hurt,' Lauri complained finally. The two of them just lay on their backs, holding their ribs from the pain, trying desperately to halt any last giggle that might

want to make its way to their pharynxes. After this inter-
lude of silence, this chuckleless reprieve, Bobby asked a
question in low monotone. It was an enquiry without
emotion, just a nagging thought. 'Why would anyone
throw a suitcase in the river?' Bobby asked.

Lauri kept the back of her head flat against the floor
and stared up at the frosted globe of the Perkinses'
entrance-hall light. That thought about the suitcase floated
through her mind, mixed with Chanel and white rabbit fur,
and she was about to speak when there came a loud slam
at the door. Lauri got a distinct flash that the answer to
all the little riddles would be soon forthcoming.

Chapter 14

Bobby sprang to the small glass peephole in his front door in time to see Mr Hulka walk past. Because of the wide-angle effect of the glass he could see for several feet to the left and to the right. Mr Hulka was wearing a coat, heading down the hall. Directly across from Bobby's door, his eye fell upon the entrance to apartment 24F and Bobby couldn't help lamenting that there were no neighbours living there, no neighbours anywhere on the floor to run to.

'What's going on?' Lauri whispered.

'*Shhh*,' was all she got for a response as Bobby's ears wiggled for a special noise. At last it came, the sound of elevator doors opening at the far end of the hall. Quickly Bobby unlocked the door and peeked out. Sure enough, Mr Hulka had got into the elevator. 'Now's our chance,' Bobby shouted, shutting the door and rushing to the terrace door. He unlocked it quickly. 'Come on,' he ordered.

By the time Lauri had reached the terrace, Bobby had already swung out and around the partition to land on the Hulkas' terrace. He motioned Lauri to follow but she wasn't about to take the elliptical orbit out over the railing. Instead, she got down on her stomach and motioned for Bobby to pull her under the small space between the bottom of the partition and the cement terrace. Once safely under, she sprang up and the two of them stared into the living-room. The curtains were open and there was Mrs Hulka, still lounging in the hammock. Bobby gave a loud rap on the window to get her attention, but Mrs Hulka did not respond.

'She's dead,' Bobby said.

'She's drunk,' Lauri corrected. 'Drunk and passed out.'

136

Her voice sounded more hopeful than convincing. Bobby yanked on the handle of the Thermopane door and to his surprise it slid right open.

'Mrs Hulka,' he called towards the figure in the hammock.

'She's just in a stupor,' Lauri insisted.

'Get to that peephole,' Bobby ordered, pointing to the Hulkas' front door.

'I will not,' Lauri said.

'You've got to get over there and keep your eye glued to it and yell if you see him coming back down the hall.'

Now that made perfect sense, enough to propel Lauri quickly across the living-room, expecting at any moment that Mrs Hulka would bolt upright and start screaming that a teenage invasion was in progress. Lauri scurried the last few feet, deciding it was really Mr Hulka they would have to worry about, and it was better that she did get to the peephole and make sure that that hall was clear.

'Nobody coming,' Lauri reported, feeling very relieved now that she could see clear down to the elevators.

Bobby approached the hammock. 'Mrs Hulka,' he repeated. 'Mrs Hulka.' Again there was no response, so he reached out his hand to give the hammock a little shake. His fingers touched Mrs Hulka's hand and instead of her skin giving like any kind of living flesh, it was stiff and hard. Bobby had touched her with more strength than he thought, or maybe it had been a reflex from the strange texture his hand had met, but before he knew what was happening the hammock began to swing and the form of Mrs Hulka began to roll. Before Bobby could stop it, her entire body flipped out of the hammock, doing a complete revolution and crashing on to the floor. Lauri turned at the impact and felt ready to faint on two counts. First, the lady that had been in the hammock was *not* Mrs Hulka, and second, the lady in the hammock had the handle of a very large beef-knife sticking out of her chest.

'Oh baby Jesus, oh baby Jesus, oh baby Jesus,' was all Lauri could say.

'Don't look,' Bobby ordered. 'Just keep your eye on the peephole and yell if you see anything coming down the hall.'

'It's not even Mrs Hulka,' Lauri said, her voice breaking.

'No, it isn't. It looks like her.'

'Then who is it?'

'You got me,' Bobby said. 'But whoever it is is very, very dead.'

Lauri zipped her eye back to the hole and used both hands on the doorknob to keep herself from falling down. She would have to forget what she had just seen. She just concentrated on the view of the hall, the rows and rows of doors to the empty apartments and the black door to the incinerator room at the far end. Most important of all, she kept her sight glued to the obtuse view of the elevator doors. That was her only job, she kept repeating to herself. Somebody was deceased. Somebody was actually deceased was the other motif that kept crawling into her consciousness, but she absolutely refused to remember that she had seen a knife jammed right in the middle of this blonde-haired woman who had been dressed in Mrs Hulka's lounging robe.

Bobby moved quickly across the living-room.

'Let's get out of here,' Lauri pleaded.

'In a minute,' Bobby said. He dashed into the bedroom hallway and disappeared from Lauri's peripheral vision.

'He'll be right back,' she called out. 'I just know he'll be coming right back.' She switched eyes so she could see when Bobby would come out of the bedroom. When he emerged he then hurried quickly into the kitchen hallway.

'There's TV parts all over the bedroom,' Bobby said. 'Picture tube and all.'

'Maybe that's what all the banging was,' Lauri said, but she didn't have enough strength in her voice for him to hear. Besides, her mouth was pointed right at the door. Lauri changed eyes again from the peephole. One could see the big RCA console. It was in a rather strange position, catty-cornered, pulled away from the wall, and much too near the front door. You'd think that if Mr Hulka had a woman with a knife in her, he had more problems than to go around yanking out the insides of a television. Actually, the RCA looked more like a big steamer trunk, about to go on a trip somewhere. That was when she also noticed the big pile of thick rope and the dripping.

'Bobby,' Lauri mumbled. 'Bobby,' she repeated with more energy.

'What?' Bobby called back with some concern from somewhere within the labyrinth of that apartment. 'Is he coming?' Lauri heard Bobby tack on.

'No.'

'Just call me as soon as you see him,' Bobby bellowed. 'We'll have plenty of time to make it back over to my place.'

Lauri renewed her eyeball contact with the peephole. But the slow drip from the console had her very curious. She stretched out her right leg and slipped her toe under the closed door where the picture tube would ordinarily be concealed. The dripping was only about a drop a minute. It seemed to be a slightly crimson colour, until it hit the purple throw rug, at which point it just sort of looked a little blackish. After a little manipulation she got the toe of her shoe under the little door of the console and yanked it from its magnetic catch until it swung wide on its hinges, and there, staring at her, pressed against the plastic screen, which should have held the picture tube, was the head of Mrs Hulka; only the head.

Lauri screamed. In a flash Bobby was next to her. He saw Mrs Hulka's head peering out of the television set. He slammed the door closed.

'Uh-oh,' Bobby said. 'Maybe this time we should get out of here.'

'I second the motion,' Lauri said.

Bobby started to help her towards the terrace when there came a noise from the hall. By now Bobby had become very used to the swooshing sound of the elevators.

He shot his eye to the peephole. 'Here he comes,' Bobby reported.

'Oh baby Jesus.' Lauri whimpered, starting to meander somewhat helplessly in the direction of the terrace door. She tried not to look at the face of the strange lady on the floor. The woman, whoever she was, had obviously been dressed up to look like Mrs Hulka and her hands had twisted themselves in the fall so that it seemed as if they were clutching the knife handle to her chest like a black lily.

'Hold it,' Bobby called sharply.

Lauri froze at the door to the terrace, but then turned at the sound of a lot of clicking.

'What are you doing?' Lauri asked. She could plainly see he was switching on all the Hulkas' locks. 'He'll know we're in here,' Lauri stressed.

'He already knows,' Bobby said. 'Take a look.'

Lauri hesitated and then moved quickly back to the peephole. There was Mr Hulka looking right at her from just a few feet outside the door. He was beautifully dressed, his handkerchief peeking neatly out of his pocket. His eyes were the only things which seemed a bit askew. The other unusual fact was that he was carrying a rather large piece of chain. He set the chain down on the floor right outside the Perkinses' apartment and went to work.

'Did you put the double lock and chain back on?' Lauri asked, knowing the answer only too well.

'No,' Bobby said, moving Lauri away from the peephole. He put his eye to the observation glass. He saw Mr Hulka take out a simple plastic card from his wallet, slip it in between the main lock and the frame of the door. A moment later there was a metallic sound. Mr Hulka had opened the door to the Perkinses' apartment and gone inside.

'He's in *my* apartment,' Bobby protested.

'He's what?' Lauri asked, feeling a shiver hopscotch down her legs and somehow end up in her throat.

'Lock the terrace door here,' Bobby ordered.

Lauri had to suspend all personal thought and ran past the corpse on the floor. In a second she was back at Bobby's side.

'If he swings around on to this terrace, we'll run out this door,' Bobby said, flicking two of the locks off.

Lauri moved closer to Bobby until she could feel his heart was banging away as loudly as hers. She didn't have to be told that her eyes were assigned to watch for any leaping figure to land on the Hulkas' terrace, any form swinging suddenly and drastically around the partition, and that Bobby's assignment was to keep his eye on that hallway. Lauri tried to keep her thoughts off Mrs Hulka's head in the TV console, but every time a drip fell it was like losing blood of her own. In a sense, in some strange way, it seemed as though everything had become as silent and dead as the dolls' houses and the line-up of Victorian dissection kits. She began to hope that Mr Hulka would leap into view on the terrace. Then they could be out the door, down the hallway, leaping whole landings. They could beat the elevator down to the lobby, that's how much glycogen she knew was pulsing through their arteries.

'Here he comes,' Bobby said hoarsely, flicking back on all the locks. 'You get over to the terrace door. He's up to something,' Bobby whispered. 'He's moving too slowly, too smoothly. It's like he's stalking a fly.'

'*Two* flies,' Lauri corrected, standing poised in the terrace doorway and getting ready to dive under the partition.

'Go,' Bobby yelled as Mr Hulka began to insert his keys into the locks, releasing them one by one, slowly, casually.

Bobby reached the terrace, slammed the glass door shut behind them and swung around the partition like a chimp. He was back on his own terrace before Lauri had even half wiggled the required distance, so he yanked her the rest of the way. She practically slid out of harm's way and in a flash they were through the Perkinses' terrace door, had it slammed and locked, and Bobby ran to the hall door, put on the double lock and chain and slid the chair into place.

'What did Hulka want in here?' Lauri asked nervously, doing a 360-degree turn of the entire junk-filled apartment.

'I don't know,' Bobby admitted. 'The one thing I do know is you call your mother and father right now and tell them we need help. Tell them to get everybody they can and get up here before we end up losing one of the favourite parts of our bodies!' Lauri winged to the in-house phone, picked up the receiver and started dialling. She dialled the entire number before she realized she hadn't heard a dial tone or any of the familiar static background. When she saw the receiver wire hanging loosely, she realized she was never going to get a dial tone, because that line was dead.

'He's cut the line,' Lauri announced, looking at the piece of wire, thinking for a moment that maybe they could splice it back together again, but then she saw that there had been two other cuts in the wires that came from the body of the wall phone itself.

Bobby took a look, froze for a moment, and then ran to the living-room. He grabbed the regular phone but he didn't have to bother dialling because he could see the floorboard terminal had been sliced off and crushed. He ran to the kitchen extension. The fashionable white push-button wall phone had been ripped right off the plaster as though it had offended some very powerful beast.

There was a moment of paralysed silence between them and then they knew, both their minds were churning like IBM computers just fed some rather depressing vital information.

'Now he wants us,' Lauri said, walking towards the sofa like a condemned prisoner. She sat down and looked at Bobby.

Bobby could see that she was on the verge of a nervous conniption, so he decided to take a more positive position on the matter. 'Nope,' he said as though it were a fact. 'He wants us to stay in here, keep our mouths shut, until he can get rid of the body and . . . so forth. As long as we sit tight, he is probably going to take that chain and the rope and tie up the TV console. He's probably got it on rollers or some guys, maybe even Pinocchio coming up from the funeral parlour, to roll it out and then stick it in the station-wagon. That's all he's doing. That's the only reason he cut the wires. He just needs the time to get rid of the evidence and then he won't care what we say because nobody believes us anyway.'

Lauri looked considerably happier at that thought. 'Do you think so?'

'Sure,' Bobby stated. 'If we don't try to make trouble, we're okay.'

'But he's a maniac,' Lauri reminded him.

'Who says?'

'Oh come on, now. Nobody puts corpses in hammocks and sticks their wife's head in an RCA.'

Bobby tried to reach for the logic involved. 'He's probably just a murderer, and you know how many murderers there are in the world. Most people don't even consider murderers crazy any more, just sort of like it's the thing to do. You can get right out on bail.'

'Oh, that's comforting,' Lauri said, finding enough energy to sit on the edge of her seat. Her legs tense, ready to run in any direction.

'At least now maybe you'll believe me,' Bobby gloated.

'Oh, I believe you. I believe you,' Lauri emphasized.

'So I'm telling you, don't worry,' Bobby insisted.

He had no idea what was really going to happen, but he figured if Lauri fainted there would be no point in even trying any kind of action. He just continued to bolster her confidence that they weren't in danger. 'You've got to understand the difference between a maniac and a murderer.'

'Why?'

'Because it explains a lot of things,' Bobby pronounced enthusiastically. 'I really saw Mr Hulka kill somebody this morning, but it wasn't Mrs Hulka. It was that blonde lady who's in the hammock now with the knife in her. She looks like Mrs Hulka, and she was the one who was wearing the white fur.'

'Oh, yes, I was going to tell you about that,' Lauri mumbled. 'I was about to tell you about that and a few odours.'

'You see, when I looked over he was choking her, and then somehow, when I was running to call you to get help and getting over to his door, he probably ran into the kitchen, grabbed a knife, jabbed it in her and then went and hid her someplace in the apartment.'

'The sauna, I'll bet,' Lauri offered.

'Right,' Bobby agreed. 'Or maybe in one of the laundry baskets. It doesn't matter. All he had to do was get that white coat on the dummy before anybody came.'

'I had wanted to tell you that that coat was too cheap for Mrs Hulka,' Lauri offered belatedly.

'I knew there was something strange about it. That's why I asked you if you noticed anything. I couldn't put my finger on it, but all murderers leave clues, and since it wasn't Mrs Hulka's coat, that's why she really laced into Mr Hulka after the police had left.'

'Oh, it was a love triangle, wasn't it?' Lauri said.

'Right,' Bobby confirmed. 'Hulka had that other woman as a girl-friend somewhere and she showed up to blackmail him.'

'Or maybe she loved him so much she finally couldn't keep it inside of her any longer and she had to come right to his apartment and confess the great feelings she had for him,' Lauri offered as an alternative possibility.

'Yeah, we can't figure out exactly what it was, but whatever, that woman must have done something that triggered off the fact that he had to kill her and then after the cops left, and we were back in the apartment here, we heard what sounded like the same thing going on again because Mrs Hulka saw the coat, she knew it wasn't hers, she got into a big fight, maybe even found the body, and we know that Mr Hulka hated her anyway – they used to fight all the time, you remember – and she was a mean piece of work,' Bobby underlined.

'Maybe she did the best she could,' Lauri suggested.

'It doesn't matter,' Bobby reminded her, 'because then he knocked the wife off, and the bottom line of this whole thing is that there's one whole body and one head over there that he's still got to get rid of. And maybe a few other pieces.'

'I'll bet it was something like that,' Lauri said, imagining that she could even still smell the cheap gardenia perfume.

'And it's Mrs Hulka's body that's in the trunk with all the metal baby hands in the Hudson,' Bobby said, feeling as though enormous wisdom was at his command. As he thought that one over he moved automatically to the terrace door, checked to make sure it was locked, and then pulled the drapes.

'What are you doing?' Lauri asked.

'I don't want him to see what we're doing in here.'

'What are we doing?'

'We're solving a crime,' Bobby explained.

Lauri looked at him quizzically. 'Bobby, we may be solving one crime but we may be about to become statistics in another.' Then Lauri had a flash. 'Why did he save her head?'

'Hulka's smart,' Bobby said. 'They can trace a body through the head, the teeth, dental records and all that stuff. All you have to do is stick the head in somebody else's coffin and have it buried at some other funeral later on, or epoxy it in a tree trunk. I mean, you read about that kind of thing every day.'

'And that's not crazy?' Lauri enquired.

'Oh, no,' Bobby assured her. 'That's called a crime of passion. When people love each other, they do all sorts of things.'

'That's very nice, but what are we supposed to do now?' Lauri complained, finding her head rotating from the front door to the terrace curtains.

'Sit tight,' Bobby instructed, 'until he gets the body

and the head out and then we're in the clear.'

'He'll get away,' Lauri complained. 'I thought you were the kid who didn't like anybody to get away with anything, no less decapitation!'

'As soon as we hear he's gone, we'll go down to your mother and father. They'll help us make such a fuss that they'll catch him,' Bobby assured her, 'unless he's already got all his money out of his bank accounts – maybe he's got shoe boxes full of money, I don't know all the kinds of tax-evasion gimmicks undertakers use. For all we know, maybe he even sold the Hulka Funeral Home, or maybe he just rents it so he doesn't have a big investment there. Sometimes even in a crime of passion, the killer has all his cash together to get out of the country,' Bobby invented, trying to make Lauri relax, his eyes all the while searching the entire room. Bobby felt his every instinct coming alive and he was looking at all of his father's tools, all of the construction equipment his mother used. Without even going into the kitchen he remembered the pot of hot water. He knew that if that wasn't enough there was even hot water that came out of the tap. He knew there were large carving knives in the kitchen drawers. He knew there were strong metal shears intended to clip the wings from roast turkeys. He knew there were cans of oven cleaners and a spice rack with pepper and even a can of Ajax. There were things in the apartment that could be used to blind or debilitate or even kill a charging madman. He sat next to Lauri on the edge of the seat. He squeezed her right knee and gave her a big wink, but he could tell that she saw through his cover. He knew his every move now was betraying the fact that he felt they were in very great danger.

Chapter 15

They were still sitting on the edge of the sofa, that middle ground between the front door and the terrace exit, when the first significant sound came. Someone was at the Perkinses' front door, someone doing something out in the hall. There was the sound of metal, the sound of a chain. The door handle began to turn as in the tradition of the best stories of haunted houses, but Bobby knew no one would be coming in because of the locks. Nevertheless he moved with Lauri over to the terrace door. He pulled aside the curtain with his hand and kept a finger ready to throw the lock switch in case – just in case – Mr Hulka had some magic trick for ripping a door off its hinges. After a few minutes the sounds in the hall stopped. Bobby let the window curtain fall back into place.

'Wait here,' Bobby said.

Lauri stood with her back against the drapes and watched as Bobby moved to the front door and carefully looked through the peephole. He made certain he could see light in the hall before moving his eye completely into place because for all he knew Hulka might have an ice pick and be ready to ram it through the tiny aperture. He stared long and hard, and then moved the chair from the knob.

'What do you see?' Lauri whispered, practically doing a two-step, feeling very strange about being so near the terrace doors. There seemed to be cold draughts creeping in all about her ankles.

'Uh-oh,' was Bobby's first response. To Lauri's amazement he suddenly began unlocking the door – everything except the chain catch – and started yanking to get the door ajar.

'What are you doing?' Lauri cried out, dumbfounded.

'He's got a chain around the outside doorknob, that chain he had – and he's anchored it to the doorknob of the apartment across the hall!' Bobby said, brimming with shock.

'What does that *mean*?' Lauri asked, clearing her throat.

'It means we can't get out the front door, that's what it means!' Bobby blurted, getting very angry. He began to pull on the doorknob like a desperate mouse in a cartoon where a cat is going to devour it if it can't get a dresser drawer open in time. 'Open the drapes!' Bobby bellowed. 'Open the drapes!' he commanded, twisting his head to look behind as he made a last series of yanks at the front door. At his order Lauri spun around and grabbed the cords which controlled the curtains. She pulled fast and hard and screamed at the top of her lungs when she found herself face to face with the towering form of Hulka, with only the glass to separate them. Bobby came flying across the room, running for all he was worth as Hulka's eyes telegraphed a message beyond hate. His hair was wet with sweat, no doubt from the effort he had to put in on linking the chain in the hall to seal that exit from them, and his lips were thin and sharp. There was something frighteningly mechanical about his stance as his right hand rose clutching a large claw hammer. Like a drummer, determined, he brought the hammer down fast and hard at the Thermopane just outside the small catch. The outer sheet of glass exploded with a deafening crash. Lauri screamed again and ran for the front door to see if she could pull it free from the anchoring chain. Bobby began to shout. 'We need help! Help!' he bellowed towards the air ducts, towards any crack or opening that flashed through his memory. There was no longer intelligent communication between him and Lauri – only instinctive. Lauri kept screaming and turned to look at the terrace door just as Mr Hulka raised his hand again, his hammer ready, letting the last piece of glass from the outer sheet fall; and then it came down again. Lauri banged on the front door, kicked it, shrieked as Bobby rushed the terrace door. Lauri knew he was throwing himself first to the beast. The hammer struck. Somehow Mr Hulka had misjudged. The inner pane was thicker and the head of the hammer only knocked out a hole the size of a plum. But something had to give further – and this time it was the hammer. The head of the hammer flew from the top of its handle like a deadly steel bird and disappeared over the edge of the terrace. Hulka rammed the handle in through the hole trying to enlarge it, but the handle split against the bulletproof-like strength of the Thermopane. Mr Hulka's fingers came through the hole now like thick evil worms and Lauri was paralysed. But not Bobby. Bobby was out in the kitchen in a flash. He came running back towards the terrace doors with the hot kettle, the kettle with the near-boiling water, and he poured some of the fluid on the groping fingers. Bobby didn't like the slow manner in which the fingers retreated. It was as though they were saying, 'We're prepared for pain; a *great deal* of pain.' Mr Hulka stood tall and straight behind the glass. His fingers advanced through the hole again, reaching for the door lock, and Bobby let another dose of the hot water fly. The fingers moved out again, away – and Bobby began to think double-time, triple-time about his choices.

'Lauri!' he called without taking his attention away from Mr Hulka's presence. 'Help me,' he ordered.

'I can't,' Lauri said. 'I'm starting to pass out.'

'Pass out later!' Bobby demanded. 'Get over here now!'

Lauri was at his side. He slipped the kettle handle into her hand and the fingers began their journey inside again, more swiftly towards the lock. Bobby realized Lauri wasn't going to react so he helped her throw the water, dousing the partial hand that would be around their throats or driving a knife into them if they didn't act.

Hulka moved his hand out even more slowly. Each time seemed to be taking more and more water from the kettle, and soon it would be empty. Bobby ran to the kitchen yelling, 'Don't let him open that lock!' He pulled open a drawer and there were the knives. He looked at the stove and the sink. He'd pull Lauri in there if Hulka got in. They'd have to fight from there. A kitchen arsenal. The blue flames on one of the burners were still lit, which gave him an idea. He ran into the living-room just as Lauri was giving Hulka's fingers another splashing of hot water.

'It's almost all gone,' Lauri complained. She found she couldn't take her eyes off Mr Hulka. Not only because she had to watch for any new tactic but also because he was so hypnotically frightening. He was still in a jacket and tie and she had the strangest feeling he was trying to mesmerize her. His craziness was paralysing her, almost drawing her to him.

Bobby was leaping over the junk in his mother's corner of the living-room. He was knocking over piles of paper and plastic constructions and books and clay busts. *Where is it*, he asked himself frantically, *what has happened to it?*

Lauri heard Bobby ploughing through the living-room and she prayed he was going to find a bazooka or something she didn't know the Perkinses owned. Mrs Perkins rendered everything into art so maybe she was doing some sort of gun collage or cannon reclamation. She watched as Mr Hulka's fingers came in through the hole in the glass once more. He seemed to be testing her beyond her position as keeper of the kettle; it was as though he was deliberately cutting his knuckles on the sharp edge of the glass, deliberately bleeding to see what effect it would have on her. Lauri let the last of the hot water fly and Mr Hulka politely withdrew his fingers. He remained hovering over her like a mammoth preserved in ice, his eyes riveting her. Suddenly there came the sound of compressed gases and Lauri turned in time to see Bobby ignite the neck of his mother's butane torch. Bobby came towards her quickly, the solitary small flame sharply focused. He almost knocked her over as the flame moved in, protecting the area around the terrace-door lock. 'Hold this,' he said.

'I can't,' she protested, but it was in her hands.

'Just hold him off for another couple of minutes and I'll have us out of here.'

'I can't,' Lauri said. 'I can't burn anybody.' But Bobby was already gone from her side. She just stood there with the flame, shadows flickering along the railing – a small flame before a giant. In her wildest self-punishing moods she couldn't have dreamed of a worse nightmare for herself and she felt herself losing consciousness. She was literally fainting, she told herself. She couldn't stand upright any longer. She even thought perhaps she was already dead. Then she saw Mr Hulka's lips move. He was speaking to her, but she couldn't hear him. He was saying words but the butane torch sounded like wind rushing through an old house and she had to move closer to the glass. She would move the torch farther down and then she might be able to comprehend.

'I was told to do it,' Mr Hulka said. Not plaintively – factually. Delicately proud.

Lauri decided it would definitely be in her and Bobby's best interests if she didn't pass out, so she tried to encourage Mr Hulka to talk. His voice was a reminder, too, that he belonged to the human species. There might be some level of reason left in him.

'*Who* told you?' Lauri asked, not certain he'd be able to hear her voice through the glass.

'That's it!' Bobby called across from the front door. 'Keep him busy.'

Lauri turned just long enough to see Bobby was working with a screwdriver on the doorknob, and then shot her attention back to Mr Hulka. 'Who told you?' she repeated.

'*Figures*,' Mr Hulka answered, coldly.

Lauri tried to draw him out. 'Figures?'

'Like in picture negatives,' Mr Hulka explained, lowering his face closer to Lauri's, his eyes seeming to see right into her soul. 'Figures who live in the dolls' houses. In the little boxes.'

Lauri lowered her gaze to the hole in the glass. Mr Hulka's fingers were only tracing the edge of it, no longer trying to enter to compete with the heat from the torch.

'I've got rid of fifty to sixty per cent of them,' Mr Hulka continued, drawing Lauri's gaze upward. 'They had infected my wife and made her sick. I've seen at least thirty-four of them. The apartment is possessed by figures; we had to keep lights burning for them – and cover some of the windows with tinfoil.'

'I've almost got the knob off!' Bobby shouted. 'Just hold him a minute longer!'

Lauri couldn't take her eyes off Mr Hulka. His voice was so easily authoritative, his madness really not so far removed from her own – the madness of unreasonable fear. She held the torch with its spitting flame and she realized she was looking into a mirror of madness and for a moment she thought she had found the key to all insanity. For just a split second she sensed that all human beings have secret voices in them, voices lurking, waiting to take control. She actually believed she understood him for just a passing moment, and *he was staring at her as though he understood her*. Mr Hulka's eyes were filled now with a great tenderness as he lowered his face closer to hers. Only the glass was between them or it would have seemed he wanted to kiss her, rather than speak. Instead he pronounced the words, 'I will leave you and the boy side by side, *hand in hand*.'

'I don't understand,' Lauri said softly.

'I am going to hurt you in the tops of your heads,' Mr Hulka said, ramming his hand through the hole in the glass and grabbing Lauri's wrist. His ripped hand closed like a vice around her, constricting its way downward and forcing her to drop the torch. Lauri cried out. Bobby turned to see her screaming, unable to pick up the torch. He ran across the living-room and he knew he would have to act swiftly and, what was worse, gamble! He grasped the bleeding fingers holding Lauri and started to bend them back. The torch was out. There wasn't time to relight it.

There was only the need to get Lauri free even if he had to stab Hulka's hand with the screwdriver. Bobby decided first to bluff and he drew the screwdriver up into the air. Slowly, he began bringing it down in a stabbing motion. Hulka didn't flinch, so Bobby allowed the blunt handle to collide with Hulka's knuckles. It was just enough to get Lauri free.

'On the double!' Bobby shouted, running back to the front door. Lauri was on his heels as Mr Hulka's hand reached the lock catch. 'This is it,' Bobby yelled, giving the loosened doorknob a yank. The knob came off in his hand; he shoved the screwdriver into the shaft hole and the door opened. As they ran into the hall there was the sound of a beast very close behind.

Bobby and Lauri made it to the exit stairs and ran down five floors before they chanced seeing what, if anything, was following them. There was no pursuer. Still they kept running down flight after flight, having a yelling conversation all the way about what must be done. 'You tell your mother and father!'

'Okay,' Lauri agreed.

'I'm telling the lobby,' Bobby bellowed. 'The whole lobby!'

When they reached the third floor Lauri ran out into the hall braying, 'The undertaker's gone bananas!' Bobby waited at the exit door until he saw Lauri had made it safely into her apartment. He thought she had come up with the most succinct expression of the event, so when he hit the lobby floor he himself went out shouting, 'The undertaker's gone bananas! The undertaker's gone bananas!!'

Bobby was so glad to see that Joe the Schmo had been relieved by Nick, the porter and night doorman. The entire evening shift was so much more sensible and Bobby could tell they believed him as he spat out the tale of Mr Hulka. The new concierge, Nick, and two other porters responded as soon as they had enough facts and were on their way to check it out. They told Bobby to just sit quietly and rest in the lobby and they'd take care of everything – and it seemed in less than five minutes Bobby was alone near the Venus fountain still mumbling, 'The undertaker's gone bananas.' His relief lasted only sixty seconds because he had underestimated Mr Hulka once before, in fact several times before, and he wasn't about to do it again. He ran to the west alcove of the lobby and ran down the stairs to the garage levels. If he knew Hulka, Hulka would still be trying to get rid of all incriminating evidence, and since he seemed to already have the TV console prepared for full loading, it was conceivable that he'd even have a set of rollers and could be loading the thing in the one vehicle he owned which could accommodate it – the station-wagon on level three. Bobby figured Hulka had three minutes tops left to get his sins out of that building. Between the Geddeses calling the cops and neighbours, and Nick and his posse storming the heights, if that station-wagon wasn't being loaded now it never would be.

Bobby entered the third level of the garage slowly, carefully. The station-wagon was there. Empty. He'd wait. If Hulka didn't show within the next couple of minutes that would mean he either ran away, got caught, or, at the very least, had to leave behind his grisly evidence which would be enough to teach Officer Petrie and a few others a thing or two. Bobby waited a full minute before it dawned on him that once again he was doing the obvious. Hulka wouldn't take the station-wagon. He'd take the Eldorado. He'd just throw the bodies in the Eldorado, drag them down in bags or sheets, and be very unpredictably chic about the whole thing. Bobby ran for the garage stairs to get up to the second level.

The Eldorado was in its spot, green and shiny. And now that time was almost up, when Bobby knew the police and the Geddeses and Nick and every law-enforcement body within a twenty-five-mile radius would be heading to the Century Tower, Bobby knew that once again he had been tricked.

Three steps at a time Bobby ran up to the first level

of the garage and there was Mr Hulka. He was already in motion, manœuvring the Volkswagen with the purple throw rug tied to the roof. He was negotiating the turn and coming into the homestretch. A single honk and Rucci would press the button in his booth and the garage door would lift. Hulka and the corpora delicti could still get away.

Chapter 16

Having sounded the alarm to the best of her ability –
knowing her mother and father had really laced it into the
police and that the police *were* on their way – Lauri went
down to the lobby so she'd have a good view of the action.
She mainly wanted to make certain that Bobby had had
as much success as she had, but she was surprised to see
the lobby empty. She looked outside at the main entrance
and that, too, was deserted – except for a man walking a
bulldog. She decided that the entire staff must be up in
24G subduing Mr Hulka and gathering up all the sanguine
things he left around the place. But something made her
stroll across the oval to see if Rucci was in his booth.
Indeed he was, reading a copy of *Mad* magazine.

'Have you seen Bobby?' Lauri asked, for the first time
not the least bit intimidated by Rucci's hoodlike appearance and speech.

'Nope,' Rucci confided without looking up, 'and I don't
want to.'

Lauri was about to turn and go back to the lobby when
she happened to look past Rucci, through the glass booth,
and something in motion caught her eye. It was a familiar
Volkswagen with a rug tied on its roof like a thick purple
blintz. And it was roaring for the garage door. Lauri felt
like she was in some horrendous tag to a James Bond film
where the villain or one of his henchmen pops up after
you think the whole thing's over. Lauri couldn't believe
her eyes when the Volkswagen squealed to a halt and
Mr Hulka was behind the wheel beeping for Rucci to press
the button to open the garage door. Rucci reached over
his hand to oblige when Lauri let out a scream which
shook Rucci so he recoiled, hitting his head against the far
side of the booth.

'Don't open the doors!' Lauri kept yelling.

Mr Hulka got out of the VW and bellowed at Rucci, 'Open the door!'

'Don't!' Lauri cried. 'He's a killer! Don't open the door!'

Rucci looked like a mouse in an approach-avoidance lab test. He didn't know if he was coming or going, with a man booming at him from one side of the booth and a girl shrieking at him from the other. Finally, Mr Hulka left his car and charged the booth. He came like a prize-fighter, ramming forward the twenty or thirty feet towards Rucci, breaking in the door with his shoulder. Rucci covered his head with the *Mad* magazine and didn't know what was going on. Lauri stood back in case Mr Hulka wanted to crash through the front of the booth as well, but as fast as she saw Mr Hulka's hand hit the button to open the garage door she saw a figure darting into the VW. The only one who was more surprised was Hulka when he ran back to his car and found Bobby Perkins was behind the wheel. Bobby had slipped into the driver's seat and had plenty of time to put the car in gear. The garage door had lifted enough and Bobby gave it the gas. The only thing that was unfortunate was that Bobby had put the stick shift into reverse. Instead of roaring out of the garage he roared back farther into the garage, almost smashing into a cement column. Hulka came running for him, but Bobby shifted into first and did a swift bypass. He was no sooner clear of Hulka and heading for the open doorway when he saw Lauri jumping up and down signalling him to stop for her. He had put a good two hundred feet between himself and Hulka so he jammed on the brakes and Lauri jumped it. Rucci was out of his damaged booth now spinning with a WHAT ME WORRY look on his face.

Bobby started around the oval at a comfortable speed, knowing Hulka would never catch him on foot. What he didn't like was that he glanced in his rearview mirror and saw Hulka pirating a Cutlass Supreme which was parked near the outside of the garage – a privilege controlled by Rucci and allowed only if the owner leaves his keys in the car. Before Bobby and Lauri knew what was happening, Hulka was squealing after them in the Cutlass.

'What are we going to do?' Lauri asked.

'Hold on,' Bobby said.

There was a chase of only modest proportions before Hulka was almost on top of them. He began to pursue them down Main Street and for a few moments it seemed as if Bobby was going to be able to lose him. That was when Bobby was severely distracted by a hand which began to creep down the front of his windshield. Every time Bobby had to hit the brakes in the slightest, more and more of an anatomy began to slide out of the rug and start down the windshield until by the time they hit the main drag the entire upper torso of the dead woman from the hammock had emerged from the purple rug on top of the car like some unpleasant filling from an éclair. If nothing else, it drew the attention of several police cars which spun around in their tracks and began to close in on the VW and Cutlass.

'Watch out!' Bobby warned, reaching one hand across to stop Lauri from bumping into the dashboard. 'We're going to crash!'

'Baby Jesus,' was all Lauri could say. 'Oh, baby Jesus.'

Bobby managed to avoid hitting anyone as the Cutlass forced him up on to the kerb. The Volkswagen came to an abrupt halt against a cement block in front of McDonald's, but regretfully the body of the blonde woman did not. She popped right out like an oversized hood ornament. The outdoor tables were completely filled with the finest and most exclusive cliques from Fort Lee High, and the screams they let out were topped only when the police finished unrolling the blanket and Mrs Hulka's head made its appearance. Mr Hulka was subdued before he could hurt Bobby or Lauri, and was one of the first of the parties involved to be taken away from the scene. Bobby loved the newspapers taking his and Lauri's pictures. He couldn't wait to see the headlines. The attention. The sensations. The ride in the patrol car together. Lights flashing. Everyone, *everyone* looking. In the back of the patrol car Bobby put his arm around Lauri and gave her a kiss.

Lauri couldn't speak.

Now that he had finally kissed her it all seemed so sudden. She had been waiting so long. But being kissed in a patrol car, perhaps, she thought that was what made it seem sudden.

'What are you thinking about?' Bobby asked.

'A poem,' Lauri said.

'About love?'

Lauri thought a moment. 'Yes.' She stayed silent in his arms and decided to think of it once more. 'A very famous poem,' she added, and she felt very much like both Snow White and the Sleeping Beauty as she whispered it to him and gave him a kiss in return.

> 'The grave's a fine and private place,
> But none, I think, do there embrace.'

Some more titles in Lions Teen Tracks:

☐ **Catch You On the Flipside** *Pete Johnson* £1.95
☐ **The Chocolate War** *Robert Cormier* £2.25
☐ **Rumble Fish** *S E Hinton* £1.95
☐ **Tex** *S E Hinton* £1.95
☐ **Breaking Up** *Frank Willmott* £1.95

All these books are available at your local bookshop or newsagent, or to order direct from the publishers, just tick the titles you want and fill in the form below.

NAME (Block letters) _____

ADDRESS _____

_____

Send to: Collins Childrens Cash Sales, PO Box 11, Falmouth, Cornwall, TR10 9EP

I enclose a cheque or postal order or debit my Visa/Mastercard to the value of the cover price plus:

UK: 60p for the first book, 25p for the second book, plus 15p per copy for each additional book ordered to a maximum charge of £1.90.

BFPO: 60p for the first book, 25p for the second book plus 15p per copy for the next 7 books, thereafter 9p per book

Overseas and Eire: £1.25 for the first book, 75p for the second book, thereafter 28p per book.

Credit card no: _____

Expiry Date: _____

Signature: _____

Lions reserve the right to show new retail prices on covers which may differ from those previously advertised in the text or elsewhere.